How to Catch
a Wild Viscount

Tessa Dare

(This novella was previously published as *The Legend of the Werestag*.)

A Note to Readers

This novella was my very first published work, and I'm delighted to make it available again for any readers who might have missed it.

The story was originally published in May 2009 under the title *The Legend of the Werestag*. I know, I know. It's the weirdest title ever! At the time, I was a new author and hoped to catch attention through the sheer strangeness of it. But this is not, and never has been, a paranormal romance—just a light-hearted, sexy Regency romance with a few twists on gothic novels. The new title, *How to Catch a Wild Viscount*, better captures that spirit.

Even years and years after writing their story, I have such fondness in my heart for Luke and Cecily. I hope you enjoy their romance. As always, thanks for reading.

Tessa

Chapter One

Autumn, 1815

WHEN THEY'D ENTERED Swinford Woods, laughing and making merry, passing around a flask of spirits "for warmth", Denny had offered a forfeit to the first hunter to spot the beast. His last bottle of apple brandy from the pressing two years past.

Well, it would appear Cecily had won. It seemed doubtful, however, that she would survive to claim her prize.

Peering through the darkness, she studied her quarry. Dark, beady eyes regarded her around an elongated nose. The curved, lethal tip of a horn glittered in the moonlight. The creature's rank, gamy odor assaulted her, even from several paces away.

The animal impatiently pawed the leaf-strewn forest floor, fixing her all the while with an offended glare. Good heavens, it was enormous. It must outweigh her by ten stone, at least.

She didn't know what to do. Should she run? Climb a tree? Feign death and hope it lost interest and went away? She'd become separated from the others some ways back—stupid, stupid. Would they even hear her, if she called?

"Denny?" she ventured. The animal cocked its head, and Cecily cleared her throat to try again. "Portia? Mr. Brooke?"

The beast shuffled toward her, great slabs of muscle flexing beneath its hoary coat.

"Not you," she told it, taking a quick step back. "Shoo. Go home."

It bristled and snarled, revealing a narrow row of jagged teeth. Moonlight pooled like liquid around its massive jaw. Good Lord, the thing was *drooling.*

Truly panicked now, she drew a deep breath and called as loud as she could. "*Denny! Help!*"

No answer.

Oh, Lord. She was going to be slaughtered, right here in the forest. Miss Cecily Hale, a lady of perfectly good breeding and respectable fortune, not to mention oft-complimented eyes, would die unmarried and childless because she'd wasted her youth pining for a man who didn't love her. She would perish here in Swinford Woods, alone and heartbroken, having received only two kisses in the entirety of her three-and-twenty years. The second of which she could still taste on her lips, if she pressed them together tightly enough.

It tasted bitter.

Luke, you unforgivable cad. This is all your fault. If only you hadn't—

A savage grunt snapped her back into the present. Cecily looked on in horror as the vile creature lowered its head, stamped the ground—

And began to charge.

God, she truly was going to die. Whose brilliant idea had it been, to go hunting a legendary beast in a cursed forest, by the light of a few meager torches and a three-quarters moon?

Oh, yes. Hers.

Three hours earlier

"MENACING CLOUDS OBSCURED the moon's silvered radiance." Portia flattened one palm against a low-slung, imaginary sky. Her voice portentous, she continued to read from the notebook. "With a mighty crack of thunder, the heavens rent. Rain lashed the crumbling abbey in unremitting torrents, and a crystalline gale blasted like the very breath of Hell."

From her chair near the hearth, Cecily checked a smile. This performance was pure Portia, right down to the dramatic toss of her unbound, jet-black mane.

"Rain filled the gargoyles' straining mouths, sluicing down to their craven talons and pooling in the Byzantine crevasses, viscous and obsidian." Portia dropped the notebook to her lap and closed her eyes, as though to savor the suspense. Then her eyes snapped open, and she tore the page from her notebook and crumpled it savagely before casting it into the fire. "Rubbish. Utter rubbish."

"It isn't rubbish," Cecily protested dutifully. Friends, after all, were supposed to support one another, and if Portia wanted to write gothic novels, Cecily would encourage her. It was gratifying to see her friend excited about something—*anything*—now that she'd emerged from her year of mourning. "It's a fine beginning," she said. "Dramatic and chilling. Truly, it gave me a little shiver."

"Perhaps there's a draft," Mr. Brooke remarked.

Portia ignored him. "Do you really think it will do?" She chewed her lip and fished a pencil from the folds of her skirt. "Maybe I should write it down again."

"You should. You most certainly should. I don't believe I've ever heard a group of sentences so . . . so very . . ."

"Wet?" The suggestion came from a shadowed corner of the drawing room.

Cecily recognized the deep, wry voice, but she refused to acknowledge the speaker. Why should she? Luke had spent the past week at Swinford ruthlessly ignoring *her*. Four years ago, during a ball at this very house, they'd been interrupted in the midst of a most intimate conversation. He'd left to join his regiment before dawn, and Cecily had spent four long years—the best years of her youth—waiting for him to return, praying God would one day give them a chance to resume that discussion.

Now he'd come back. They'd been in the same house for eight days. And he'd made it perfectly, painfully clear he had nothing whatever to say.

Well, she supposed she must be fair. He had spoken the word "wet" just now.

"Atmospheric," she said evenly, forbidding any note of impatience or frustration or bitter heartbreak to tweak her voice. "I was going to say it's very atmospheric."

Portia looked to their host. "Denny, what did you think?"

Cecily shot him a pleading glance. She and Denny had practically grown up together, and she knew him well enough to recognize the peril in Portia's question. He was a good-hearted, uncomplicated man, and he had a way of being too honest at times, without realizing it. *Come on, Denny. Give her a kind word. A convincing one.*

"Capital," he exclaimed, rather too loudly to sound sincere. "First rate, I'm sure. At least, I know I could never write a thing to touch it, what with the torrents and the sluicing and those Byzantine crevasses."

Portia pinched the bridge of her nose. "Lord. It *is* rubbish."

"If you want my opinion . . ." Brooke said, lifting a decanter of whiskey.

"I don't."

Brooke, of course, was undeterred. To the contrary, a keen anticipation lit his eyes. The man possessed a cutting wit, and used it to draw blood. Some gentlemen angled trout while on holiday; others shot game. Arthur Brooke made it a sport to disenchant—as though it were his personal mission to drive fancy and naiveté to extinction.

He said smugly, "My dear Mrs. Yardley, you have assembled a lovely collection of words."

Portia eyed him with skepticism. "I don't suppose that's a compliment."

"No, it isn't," he answered. "Pretty words, all, but there are too many of them. With so many extravagant ornaments, one cannot make out the story beneath."

"I can make out the story quite clearly," Cecily protested. "It's nighttime, and there is a terrific storm."

"There you have it," Denny said. "It was a dark and stormy night." He made a generous motion toward Portia. "Feel free to use that. I won't mind."

With a groan, Portia rose from her chair and swept to the window. "The difficulty is, this is *not* a dark and stormy night. It is clear, and well-lit by the moon, and unseasonably warm for autumn. Terrible. I was promised a gothic holiday to inspire my literary imagination, and Swinford Manor is hopeless. Mr. Denton, your house is entirely too cheerful and maintained."

"So sorry to disappoint," Denny said. "Shall I instruct the housekeeper to neglect the cobwebs in your chambers?"

"That wouldn't be nearly enough. There's still that sprightly toile wallpaper to contend with—all those gamboling lambs and frolicking dairymaids. Can you imagine, this morning I found myself humming! I expected this house to be decrepit, lugubrious . . ."

"Lugubrious." Brooke drawled the word into his whiskey. "Another pretty word, lugubrious. More than pretty. Positively voluptuous with vowels, lugubrious. And spoken with such . . . mellifluence."

Portia flicked him a bemused glance.

He added, "One pretty word deserves another, don't you think?"

"I don't suppose that's a compliment."

"This time it is." He raised his glass to her. "But if it's gothic inspiration you seek, Mrs. Yardley, I suggest you look to our companion." He swiveled to face Luke's corner. "Lord Merritt, I must say you are the picture of decrepitude. Lugubrious, indeed."

Luke said nothing.

Did they teach men that in the army? Cecily wondered. Drill them in the practice of cold, perfect silence? Years ago, he'd been so open and engaging. So easy to speak with. It was one of the things she'd most lov—

No. She must not use that word, not any longer.

"Actually," said Portia, giving Luke an assaying look, "with that dark, ruffled hair; the possessive sprawl of his limbs . . . I would say he is the picture of gothic intrigue and raw animal magnetism." With a dramatic sigh, she returned to her chair. "That's it. I shall put aside my novel for the evening and work on my list instead."

"Your list?" Denny asked. "What kind of list?"

"My list of potential lovers."

Cecily coughed. "Portia, surely you don't . . ."

"Oh, surely I do. I am no longer in mourning. I am a widow now, financially and otherwise independent, and I intend to make the most of it. I shall write scandalous novels and take a dozen lovers."

"All at once?" Brooke quipped.

"Perhaps in pairs," she retorted, without missing a beat.

The two locked gazes in challenge, and Cecily did not miss the current of attraction that passed between them. *Portia, be careful.* She knew her friend's salacious plans to be nine-tenths brave talk. But Brooke could take that last tenth, her vulnerable, lonely heart, and slice it to ribbons.

"Luke Trenton, the Viscount Merritt," Portia said, scribbling in her notebook. She gave Brooke a spiteful glare. "We widows do favor those dark, haunted types."

No. She wouldn't. She couldn't possibly be so obtuse. During all the years Luke was at war, Cecily had never told Portia of her hopes—she'd scarcely dared admit them to herself—but surely her friend must know her well enough to understand, to intuit . . .

"I thank you for the compliment, Mrs. Yardley," Luke said from the shadows.

No. He wouldn't. He couldn't possibly be so cruel.

"Actually, Portia," Cecily said, determined to cauterize this vein of conversation, "you may find gothic inspiration in the neighborhood, if not within the house. Denny, tell her that story you used to tell me when we were children, summering here."

His brow creased, and he ruffled his sandy hair. "The one about the vinegar bottle?"

"No, no. The one about the woods that border Corbinsdale."

"Corbinsdale?" Brooke asked. "Isn't that the Earl of Kendall's estate?"

"The very one," Denny said. "And well done, Cecily. Now *that* is a story for Portia's gothic novel."

"I don't know about my novel," Portia said, scribbling again, "but the Earl of Kendall definitely goes on the list."

"Now wait," Luke protested, "I cease to be complimented, if you're lumping me in with that old devil." He eased his chair into the firelight, and Cecily could not divert her gaze in time. Or perhaps she simply could not bring herself to look away. Portia was right; he did look haunted. Haunted, haggard, in perpetual need of a shave. The rough suggestion of a beard covered a sharply angled jaw and crept up gaunt, hollow cheeks. His face seemed more shadow than substance now. And his eyes . . . She could scarcely make out the green anymore, through that persistent glaze of liquor. When their gazes met, she saw only the pupils: two hard, black lodestones that trapped her gaze, pulled the air from her lungs, drew on her heart.

Oh, Luke. What has happened to you?

He turned away.

"The old devil you refer to died almost a year ago," Denny informed him. "The son's inherited now. A good enough fellow."

"So the ladies report." Portia flashed a wicked smile as she underscored Lord Kendall's name in her book. "He's quite a favorite with the widows, you know. Oh, Mr. Denton, do invite him for dinner!"

"Can't. He's not in residence at Corbinsdale. Never is, this time of year."

"Pity," said Brooke dryly.

"Indeed," Portia sighed. "My list is back to one."

"Leave him alone." Cursing her unthinking response, Cecily added, "Lord Kendall, I mean. And do put away your list. Denny was about to tell his story."

Luke moved to the edge of his armchair. Those cold, dark eyes held her captive as he posed a succinct, incisive question. "Jealous, Cecy?"

Cecy. No one had called her that in years. Not since that last night before he'd left, when he'd wound a strand of her hair about his finger and leaned in close, with that arrogant, devastating smile teasing one corner of his mouth. *Won't you miss me, Cecy?*

Four years later, and her blood still responded just as fiercely as it had that night, pounding in her heart and pushing a hot blush to her throat.

She *had* missed him. She missed him still.

"Don't be ridiculous," she said, deliberately misunderstanding him. "Why should I be jealous of Lord Kendall?"

"Yes, how absurd." Portia gave a throaty laugh. "Everyone knows Cecily's going to marry Denny."

Lifting his tumbler of whiskey, Luke retreated into the shadows. "Do they?"

Was it disappointment she detected in his voice? Or merely boredom? And for heaven's sake, why couldn't she simply forbid herself to care?

"Denny, won't you tell Portia the story? Please. It's so diverting." She forced a bright tone, even as tears pricked her eyes.

"As you wish." Denny went to the hearth and stirred the fire, sending up a plume of orange sparks. "The tale begins well before my time. It's common knowledge, among the locals, that the woods stretching between Swinford and Corbinsdale are cursed."

"Cursed," Brooke scoffed. "Ignorance and superstition are the true curses. Their remedy is education. Don't you sponsor a school on this estate, Denny?"

"It's a story," Portia said. "Even schoolchildren know the difference. And they could teach you something about imagination. Your cynicism is not only tiresome, but pitiable."

"You pity me? How amusing."

"Pity won't get you on my list."

"Really?" Brooke smirked. "It seems to have worked for Lord Merritt."

Enough. Cecily leapt to her feet. "A man-beast!" she exclaimed, gesturing wildly toward the windows. "There's a fiendish creature living in those woods, half man and half beast!"

There, now she had everyone's attention. Even Luke's, for the first time all week. He was regarding her as though she were a madwoman, but still.

Denny pouted. "Really, Cecily. I was getting to that."

She gave him an apologetic shrug. She was sorry to ruin the end of his story, but it was what he deserved for dithering so.

"A man-beast?" Portia asked, her eyes widening. "Oh, I do like the sound of this." She put pencil to paper again.

Brooke leaned over her shoulder. "Are you taking notes for your novel or adding to your list?"

"That depends," she said coolly, "on what manner of beast we're discussing." She looked to Denny. "Some sort of large, ferocious cat, I hope? All fangs and claws and fur?"

"Once again I must disappoint you," Denny replied. "No fangs, no claws. It's a stag."

"Oh, *prongs*! Even better." More scribbling. "What do they call this . . . this man-beast? Does it have a name?"

"Actually," said Denny, "most people in the region avoid speaking of the creature at all. It's bad luck, they say, just to mention it. And a sighting of the beast . . . well, that's an omen of death."

"Excellent. This is all so inspiring." Portia's pencil was down to a nub. "So is this a creature like a centaur, divided at the waist? Four hooves and two hands?"

"No, no," Cecily said. "He's not half man, half beast in that way. He transforms, you see, at will. Sometimes he's a man, and other times he's an animal."

"Ah. Like a werewolf," Portia said.

Brooke laughed heartily. "For God's sake, would you listen to yourselves? Curses. Omens. *Prongs*. You would honestly entertain this absurd notion? That Denny's woods are overrun with a herd of vicious man-deer?"

"Not a herd," Denny said. "I've never heard tell of more than one."

"We don't know that he's vicious," Cecily added. "He may be merely misunderstood."

"And we certainly can't call him a man-deer. That won't do at all." Portia chewed her pencil thoughtfully. "A werestag. Isn't that a marvelous title? *The Curse of the Werestag*."

Brooke turned to Luke. "Rescue me from this madness,

Merritt. Tell me you retain some hold on your faculties of reason. What say you to the man-deer?"

"Werestag," Portia corrected.

Luke circled the rim of his glass with one thumb. "A cursed, half-human creature, damned to an eternity of solitude in Denny's back garden?" He shot Cecily a strange, fleeting glance. "I find the idea quite plausible."

Brooke made an inarticulate sound of disgust.

"There's a bright moon tonight. And fine weather." Portia put aside her pencil and book, a merry twinkle shining in her eyes. Cecily recognized that twinkle. It spoke of daring, and imprudent adventure.

Which suited Cecily fine. If she had to endure this miserable tension much longer, she would grow fangs and claws herself. Imprudent adventure seemed a welcome alternative. With a brave smile, she rose to her feet. "What are we waiting for? Let's go find him."

Chapter Two

$\mathcal{A}$T LAST, CECILY had him cornered.

The party had dispersed to prepare for their impromptu hunting excursion. Brooke and Denny had gone to see about footmen and torches. Cecily was supposed to be fetching a cloak and sturdier boots from her chambers, as Portia had done, but she'd tarried purposely until the three of them had left. Until she was alone with Luke. It was time to end this . . . this foolish dream she'd been living for years.

She cleared her throat. "Will you come with us, out to the woods?"

"Are you going to marry Denny?" He spoke in an easy, conversational tone. As though his answer depended on hers.

She briefly considered chastising his impudence, refusing to answer. But why not give an honest reply? He'd already made her humiliation complete, by virtue of his perfect indifference. She could sink no lower by revealing it. "There is no formal understanding between us. But everyone assumes I will marry him, yes."

"Because you are so madly in love?"

Cecily gave a despairing sniff. "Please. Because we are cousins of some vague sort, and we can reunite the ancestral fortune." She stared up at the gilt ceiling trim. "What else would people assume? For what other earthly reason would I have remained unmarried through four seasons? Certainly not because I've been clinging to a ridiculous infatuation all this time. Certainly not because I've wasted the best years of my youth and spurned innumerable suitors, pining after a man who had long forgotten me. No, no one would ever credit that reasoning. They could never think me such a ninny as *that*."

That cold, empty silence again. A sob caught in her throat.

"Was there anything in it?" she asked, not bothering to wipe the tear tracing the rim of her nose. "Our summer here, all those long walks and even longer conversations? When you kissed me that night, did it mean anything to you?"

When he did not answer, she took three paces in his direction. "I know how proud you must be of those enigmatic silences, but I believe I deserve an answer." She stood between his icy silence and the heated aura of the fire. Scorched on one side, bitterly cold on the other—like a slice of toast someone had forgotten to turn.

"What sort of answer would you like to hear?"

"An honest one."

"Are you certain? It's my experience that young ladies vastly prefer fictions. Little stories, like Portia's gothic novel."

"I am as fond of a good tale as anyone," she replied, "but in this instance, I wish to know the truth."

"So you say. Let us try an experiment, shall we?" He rose from his chair and sauntered toward her, his expression one of jaded languor. His every movement a negotiation between aristocratic grace and sheer brute strength.

Power. He radiated power in every form—physical, intellectual, sensual—and he knew it. He knew that she sensed it.

The fire was unbearably warm now. Blistering, really. Sweat beaded at her hairline, but Cecily would not retreat.

"I could tell you," he said darkly, seductively, "that I kissed you that night because I was desperate with love for you, overcome with passion, and that the color of my ardor has only deepened with time and separation. And that when I lay on a battlefield bleeding my guts out, surrounded by meaningless death and destruction, I remembered that kiss and was able to believe that there was something of innocence and beauty in this world, and it was you." He took her hand and brought it to his lips. Almost. Warm breath caressed her fingertips. "Do you like that answer?"

She gave a breathless nod. She was a fool; she couldn't help it.

"You see?" He kissed her fingers. "Young ladies prefer fictions."

"You are a cad." Cecily wrenched her hand away and balled it into a fist. "An arrogant, insufferable cad."

"Yes, yes. Now we come to the truth. Shall I give you an honest answer, then? That I kissed you that night for no other reason than that you looked uncommonly pretty and fresh, and though I doubted my ability to vanquish Napoleon, it was some balm to my pride to conquer you, to feel you tremble under my touch? And that now I return from war, to find everything changed, myself most of all. I scarcely recognize my surroundings, except . . ." He cupped her chin in his hand and lightly framed her jaw between his thumb and forefinger. "Except Cecily Hale still looks at me with stars in her eyes, the same as she ever did. And when I touch her, she still trembles."

Oh. She *was* trembling. He swept his thumb across her cheek, and even her hair shivered.

"And suddenly . . ." His voice cracked. Some unrehearsed emotion pitched his dispassionate drawl into a warm, expressive whisper. "Suddenly, I find myself determined to keep this one thing constant in my universe. Forever."

She swallowed hard. "Do you intend to propose to me?"

"I don't think so, no." He caressed her cheek again. "I've no reason to."

"No reason?" Had she thought her humiliation complete? No, it seemed to be only beginning.

"I'll get my wish, Cecy, whether I propose to you or not. You can marry Denny, and I'll still catch you stealing those starry looks at me across drawing rooms, ten years from now. You can share a bed with him, but I'll still haunt your dreams. Perhaps once a year on your birthday—or perhaps on mine— I'll contrive to brush a single fingertip oh-so-lightly between your shoulder blades, just to savor that delicious tremor." He demonstrated, and she hated her body for responding just as he'd predicted.

An ironic smile crooked his lips. "You see? You can marry anyone or no one. But you'll always be mine."

"I will not," she choked out, pulling away. "I will put you out of my mind forever. You are not so very handsome, you know, for all that."

"No, I'm not," he said, chuckling. "And there's the wonder of it. It's nothing to do with me, and everything to do with you. I know you, Cecily. You may try to put me out of your mind. You may even succeed. But you've built a home for me in your heart, and you're too generous a soul to cast me out now."

She shook her head. "I—"

"Don't." With a sudden, powerful movement, he grasped her waist and brought her to him, holding her tight against his chest. "Don't cast me out."

His mouth fell on hers, hard and fast, and when her lips parted in surprise, he thrust his tongue deep into her mouth. He kissed her hungrily, thoroughly, without finesse or restraint, as though he hadn't kissed a woman in years and might not survive to kiss another tomorrow. Raw, undisguised need shuddered through his frame as he took from her everything he could—her inhibitions, her anger, her very breath.

And still she yearned to give him more. Arching on tiptoe, she threaded her hands into his hair and boldly touched her tongue to his. She'd been afraid to, the last time. But she wasn't afraid now, and she wasn't satisfied with a timid, schoolgirl kiss. Her body bowed into his, and he moaned as he kissed her deeper still. This was what she'd been dreaming of, for so long. His taste, his warmth, his strength surrounding her. This was Luke.

This was *Luke*.

The man who'd years ago held her, kissed her, and left her in the morning without so much as an *adieu*. The man who saw no reason to marry her now. He was just going to do it all again. Hold her, kiss her . . . then leave her alone and yearning for him. Forever.

She pushed against his shoulders, breaking the kiss. "Luke—"

"Cecy," he murmured, his mouth falling to the underside of her jaw. He burrowed into the curve of her neck, licking her pulse, catching her earlobe between his teeth . . .

17

"Luke, no." Her voice was thick.

His hand slid up to roughly clutch her breast, and he nipped her ear, hard. Pain and pleasure shot through her, and she dug her fingernails into his neck. For a mad moment, she wanted to bite him too. To punish him, mark him . . . to taste him one more time.

"Stop." She fisted her hands in his hair and tugged. "*Stop*."

He froze, then slowly raised his head. His lips still held the shape of a kiss, and she slapped his cheek hard enough to make them go slack.

"Stop," she repeated clearly. "I won't let you do this to me again."

He blinked, slowly relinquishing his grip on her breast. Then releasing her entirely.

Cecily knew better than to expect an apology. She smoothed the front of her gown. "I ought to have Denny cast you out of this house."

"You should." Luke stared at her, rubbing his jaw with one hand. "But you won't."

"You think you know me so well? It's been four years. I'm not that naïve, infatuated girl any longer. People change."

"Some people do. But not you."

"Just watch me, Luke." She backed out of the room. "Just watch me."

LUKE WATCHED FROM his bedchamber window as the would-be-gothic, all-too-comic hunting party sallied forth. Footmen bearing torches flanked the four adventurers: Intrepid Denny in the lead; the dark-haired Portia and slender Brooke a few paces behind, squabbling as they went. Cecily, with her flaxen hair and dove-gray cloak, bringing up the rear—graceful, pensive, lovely. She'd always worn melancholy well. She was rather like the moon that way: a fixture of bright, alluring sadness that kept watch with him each night.

No, she had not changed. Not for him.

He watched as the "hunters" crested a small rise at the edge of the green. On the downslope, Cecily made a brisk surge forward and took Denny's arm. Then together they disappeared, the green-black shadows of the forest swallowing them whole.

Luke felt no desire to chase after them. He'd had his fill of tramping through cold, moonlit forests—forests, and mountain ranges, and picked-clean orchards and endless fallow fields. He was weary of marching, and bone-tired of battle. Yet if he wanted Cecily, it seemed he must muster the strength to fight once more.

Did he truly want to win?

The answers were supposed to come to him here. Here at Swinford Manor, where they'd spent that idyllic summer, racing ponies and reading *Tom Jones* and rolling up the carpet to dance reels in the hall. When Denny had invited him back for this house party, Luke had eagerly accepted. He'd supposed he would greet Cecily, kiss her proffered hand and simply know what to do next. Things had always been easy between them, before. And the way he saw it, the pertinent questions were simple, and few:

Did she still care for him?

Did he still want her?

Yes, and yes. God, yes.

And yet nothing was easy between them, and Cecily had questions of her own.

When you kissed me that night, did it mean anything to you? How could he give her an honest answer? When he'd kissed her that night, it *had* meant little. But there'd been moments in the years since—dark, harrowing, nightmarish moments—when that kiss had come to mean everything. Hope. Salvation. A reason to drag one mud-caked boot in front of the other and press on, while men around him fell. He had remembered Cecily, in times and places he hadn't expected to think of her at all. In places a delicate, well-bred lady had no business intruding. He'd dragged that memory—that fresh, pure kiss—through muck, sweat, blood. Surely he'd sullied it, tainted her innocent affection with violence and raw physical need. His behavior tonight had proved that beyond any doubt. He'd sniped at her and insulted her, provoked her to tears. Embraced her not to offer affection or comfort, but only because a twisted spear of aggression drove him to claim her body for his own.

He'd bitten her, for Christ's sake.

People change, she'd said.

Yes, dear Cecily. They do, indeed. In more ways than you could dream.

A hollow laugh rattled in his chest. Portia had pulled them all out to the forest, to hunt for her fabled "werestag"? Little did she know, they'd left the true beast here at the house. He'd been prowling this bedchamber every night, driven wild by the knowledge only two oaken doors and some fifty paces of wainscoted corridor lay between him and the woman he'd crossed a continent to hold. By day, he'd been drinking himself into a stupor, positioning himself at the opposite end of every room, adopting a temporary vow of silence. Futile efforts, all. He'd known a scene like tonight's was coming, and he'd known it would end with Cecily hurting and in tears. Charm, politesse, gentlemanly behavior—they'd long ago been stripped away. He was down to his basest form now, both hardened and desperate, and if she had not slapped him cold this evening, only the devil knew what he would have done to her. Cecily was far safer roaming a cursed forest with Denny.

She was safer with Denny, in general.

Sighing heavily, Luke closed the velvet drapes. He tugged his cravat loose, then rang for his valet and poured himself yet another tumbler of whiskey.

Time to be honest. He did know what to do about Cecily. The answer *was* easy, and there was just enough human decency left in him to divine it. He'd known it the moment he'd pressed his cracked, weathered lips to her pale, delicate fingers eight days past.

He had to let her go.

LUKE FOLLOWED HER into the forest.

Cecily tried to leave him behind, but she couldn't. The memories stalked her down the root-scored pathways; her thoughts cast long, flickering shadows. Two kisses they'd shared now: one innocent and fresh, one desperate and demanding. Both intoxicating. Stirring, in ways she scarcely had words to describe. She'd wanted him, even as a girl, though she'd hardly known what it meant. Now a woman, she understood longing and claimed more than a passing acquaintance with desire. And she burned for him, body and soul. She must find some way to extinguish that fire, before it consumed her completely.

"Tell us more about the werestag," Portia called to Denny.

It took Cecily a moment to understand what her friend meant, and to recall that they were not hunting Luke in the undergrowth.

"Is the legend centuries old?" Portia asked, stepping over a fallen branch.

"Not at all," Denny answered. "Mere decades. If you believe the locals, these woods have been cursed for generations, but the man-beast is only one of the more recent victims."

"Oh, come now." Brooke swatted an insect against his neck, then squinted at his hand before wiping it against his trousers. "What evidence is there for this supposed curse? Unless by 'cursed' you mean plagued by midges, in which case I readily capitulate."

"People have died here," Cecily said.

"People die everywhere."

"Yes, but this forest claims more than its share," Denny said, pausing and raising his torch high. "And it has a taste for the young and foolhardy."

"Of course it does," Brooke argued. "Most people who die of accidental causes *are* young and foolhardy."

Denny shrugged. "Believe what you will. But there is no way to disclaim the fact that nearly every family in the area has been touched by some tragedy that occurred here. Even aristocracy cannot escape the curse. Why, the old Earl of Kendall's—"

"This local history is all so very fascinating," Portia interrupted, taking Denny's other arm, "but could we return to the story of the werestag? If we're going to find him, we ought to know what we're about."

"Yes, of course."

Denny began to tell the story, and Cecily purposefully fell a few paces behind. She'd heard this tale before, many times. How an impoverished man, desperate to feed his ailing wife and children, had gone into the forest at night to trap game. Such poaching was illegal and incurred stiff penalties, but Denny's grandfather had generally turned a blind eye to the practice. The man in the story, however, had made the grave mistake of wandering across the Corbinsdale border, and the old Earl of Kendall did not share Mr. Denton's leniency. Men had been sentenced to hard labor, even transportation, for the offense of poaching on Kendall land.

"So there he was," she heard Denny recounting in a dramatic tone, "crouched over his brace of pheasants, when he heard the hounds. The Corbinsdale gamekeeper had spotted him. The poor fellow ran, even dodged a bullet or two, weaving through the woods. But he couldn't outrun the dogs forever. He tried throwing them the pheasants, but the hounds were well trained and barely stopped to sniff at the birds."

Denny paused, drew up, considered. At length, he pointed right. "There's a deer trail, just here. We'll follow it."

Although the winding ribbon of trail was only wide enough for one, Portia clung to Denny's arm. "What did he do? The hunter, being chased by the dogs?"

"Ah, yes. Just as the dogs were about to reach him, the man fell to his knees and pleaded with the spirits of the forest to spare his life."

"And . . .?"

"And a strange force struck him to the ground, and when

his consciousness returned—he'd been transformed into a stag. A white one, so the story goes."

"Absurd," Brooke grumbled.

"After that, he easily outran the dogs—made it all the way back to Denton land. He was even able to change back into human form, once the danger had passed. But the spirits had played a cruel trick on him, you see—for he could never leave the woods again. Every time he tried to set a foot—or hoof—beyond the woodland border, some mystical force would throw him back. The forest spirits saved his life, but now they will not relinquish it."

"What of his family?" Portia asked.

"His wife died," Denny answered. "The orphaned children were sent to a workhouse. And the man-beast"—he cleared his throat—"beg pardon, *werestag*, has been doomed to roam the forest ever since."

"Rubbish. Poppycock. Lies, all of it lies." Brooke strode to the lead, then halted and turned to face the group. Everyone tripped to a standstill. "Legends," he continued, "always have a logical explanation. This is clearly a cautionary tale, concocted by old, toothless grandmothers. Everyone knows the old earl was rabid about hunting, and he had these woods stocked with exotic game—peacock, boar, and yes, even stag. Everyone knows his lands were a magnet for poachers, and that he dealt with trespassers harshly. Of course the locals created this man-deer nonsense. They wanted to scare young people, discourage them from wandering off into the woods."

"Well, if that was their intent"—Cecily looked around the group—"it doesn't seem to have worked."

"That's right." Portia released Denny's arm and continued

on the path. "Here we are, plunging ever deeper into these cursed woods, unarmed and intrigued. Fearless."

Brooke grabbed her elbow. "A thin line separates boldness from stupidity."

"Yes." Smiling sweetly, Portia looked at his hand on her arm. "You're treading it."

His lips thinned as he released her.

With an affable grin, Denny pulled out his flask. "I don't know about you all, but I'm having a capital time."

The group forged ahead in silence. Once again, Cecily let herself fall behind, the better to indulge her maudlin humor. She trailed them by ten paces or so, lingering in that auditory border between her companions' crunching footsteps and the forest's profound hush. The sounds were smaller here. The chirp of insects. The subtle cracks as tree limbs splintered overhead. Little currents of rustling that betrayed nocturnal creatures burrowing in the undergrowth. Somewhere far in the distance a confused rooster crowed, a good five hours premature. That happened, sometimes, when the moon was nearly full and so bright.

Cecily strained her ears. Could one *hear* moonlight? She almost imagined she could—one clear, silvery note ringing through the woods, like the hum of a celestial tuning fork. The sort of sound one felt in her bones, rather than detected with her ears.

Beautiful.

A bright flash caught her eye, like a distant bolt of mercury. She swiveled, tracking it left. It disappeared, and she froze, peering hard into the woods in the direction she'd seen it last. To the left, then up a slight rise . . .

There. There it was again. An arrow of white bounding through the shadows. And . . . could that sharp glint be a *prong*?

She turned and stepped toward it instinctively, then looked down in surprise when her boot failed to create the expected crunch. She'd assumed, in stepping off the path, she'd crush a goodly number of leaves and twigs beneath her heel.

But she hadn't, because the smooth-packed furrow of the trail split here, directly under her boots. The right fork led toward Denny and the rest, now several paces ahead. The left path shot off in the direction of the mysterious silver-white flash.

A thin line separates boldness from stupidity.

Yes, and she'd crossed it four years ago.

The little laugh she gave surprised her, as did the ease with which she made a choice. The decision smacked of petulance and self-destructive tendencies. Cecily knew it.

She turned left anyhow.

Chapter Three

*H*E WAITED FOR her.

There was no other possible explanation. The stag must have waited for her, patiently gleaming in the moonlight, while she followed the serpentine path through the woods. For after following the trail for just a few minutes, Cecily rounded a tight thicket of brambles to nearly collide with the beast.

He did not bolt, but stood his ground. Awed, she did the same. She fought to keep her breathing steady, to make no sudden movements. How curious, that after all the cautionary tales of a cursed man-beast—"Werestag," she heard Portia correcting in her mind—Cecily was concerned about frightening *him*.

With a soft snort, the animal gave her his handsome profile and regarded her with one large, dark, intelligent eye. His creamy hide bunched shaggy and soft on the underside of his throat, then stretched taut over his backbone and haunches. One of his rear hooves stamped the ground, as though the power coiled in those haunches wanted to spring free.

Feeling a little bit silly—and why should she, she talked to horses and dogs all the time—she addressed him. "Can you understand me? My speech, I mean?" When he gave no response, she added, "If you can understand me, nod your head twice. Or tap your hoof, perhaps."

His neck lengthened a fraction, so that his regal crown of antlers struck an even more impressive silhouette. *I am not one of your horses or dogs*, his proud bearing told her. *I do not nod or tap on command.*

Oh, yes. He understood her. Or rather, they understood one another.

A sense of affinity passed between them, a moment of mutual admiration and respect. Cecily's fingers itched to stroke the felty thatch beneath his ear, to judge if it was really as soft as it looked. But she sensed it would offend him, to be petted in such a manner.

Then off he darted again, and she stared after him, entranced by the power and grace in his easy, bounding gait. The creature halted on a distant rise, his sleek form just an iridescent glimmer in the distance.

Twice more they played this dash-and-follow game, until she was certain they must be well into Corbinsdale land. The distance didn't concern Cecily. The path was always there, to lead her back.

But then the path grew fainter. Until she wasn't even sure she was following a trail anymore, but perhaps only tracing a dried-up rill. She could hear the stream gurgling in the distance. That same stream emerged from the woods into Denny's south meadows, where they sometimes picnicked on pleasant afternoons.

A rancid odor filled the small depression where she'd halted—as though something were rotting nearby. A little shiver of nerves swept her, but she bade herself to stay calm and survey her surroundings.

She pivoted slowly. A copse of alder crowded her view, and the stag's shining form had disappeared. But she was not lost. If she had no other alternative, she could follow the stream to those familiar meadows, then return to Swinford Manor from there. It would make for a long walk home, and a muddy one, but she had several hours of good moonlight left, and a warm cloak. There was no cause for alarm. She was in no danger of wandering aimlessly in the woods until she died of thirst or starvation.

A harsh grunt made her jump.

No, she was in danger of perishing in this very spot.

Cecily turned toward the ominous snuffling noise. There, in the underbrush, lurked a boar. She'd never seen a boar, but she knew this must be one—else it was the largest, hairiest, most foul-smelling and predatory pig she'd ever encountered.

"Denny?" she called. Then, louder: "Portia? Mr. Brooke?"

The malodorous thing shuffled closer. It was drooling. Slobbering and snorting. The beast's rubbery lips quivered and curled, revealing a pair of sharp, menacing tusks to complement the smaller, hooked set bracketing his snout.

"Go away," she told it. "Shoo."

No response.

A cloud moved across the moon, painting the forest a darker shade of greenish-gray.

"*Denny! Help!*"

As the beast lowered its head and began to charge, thoughts rioted in Cecily's brain. Regrets, mostly. Of all the disgusting, miserable, lonely ways to die, she would end like this? And though she knew she had no one to blame but herself for this predicament, she felt an unreasoned surge of anger toward Luke. If he cared for her the slightest bit, she wouldn't be here at all.

That irrational stab of fury broke her silence. She had already stood up to one brute this evening. She would not go quietly now.

"Arrogant, insufferable *cad*!" she screamed at the boar, grabbing up a fallen branch and raising it high above her head. Widening her stance, she braced for the impact, forcing herself to be patient . . . wait . . . She would only have one chance, one swing.

A benevolent gust of wind whipped the hair out of her face. She focused her gaze on one flattened, bristled ear and tightened her grip.

Almost . . . almost . . .

Now.

Just as she swung, some unseen force tackled Cecily from the side. She felt herself lifted effortlessly, then hurled to the ground. The stick clattered from her grasp. Loamy soil clotted against her cheek, and her fingernails scrabbled in moss and decaying leaves.

She struggled to rise, but a heavy weight held her pinned against the ground. Was it the boar? It couldn't be. She felt no bristles against her flesh, and it didn't smell nearly bad enough. She tried to scream, but a hand clamped over her mouth.

A hand. Yes. Fingers, palm, thumb. Human.

"Be still," a deep voice growled.

And then the boar was upon them both.

Cecily's face slammed against the turf again as the beast's second charge hit home. Despite the jolt, she was aware of the stranger's frame surrounding her body, absorbing the worst of the blow. When the boar eased off, presumably to charge again, the stranger released Cecily's mouth, grabbed the tree branch she had dropped, and rolled over swinging. Even with her face still pressed into the dirt, she heard a dull crack and a porcine squeal of pain that told her the club had hit its mark.

The man's weight was gone from her now, and she rolled onto her back, propping herself up on one elbow. A few paces away, the stranger—her protector—staggered to his feet and squared off against the angry boar. With the crosshatch of branches overhead and the clouds obscuring the moon, Cecily could barely make out the forms of man and beast as they circled one another, much less make out the stranger's face.

"Denny?" she asked tentatively. His build appeared different from Denny's, but then it was dark and difficult to see. "Denny, is that you?"

The man gave no response. Really, how could he, with the boar charging him again?

Survival first, she chided herself. *Introductions later.*

The stranger dodged right and swung, clouting the beast on the ear with his club. Amidst the boar's angry squeals, Cecily registered the sound of ripping fabric and a masculine grunt of pain.

"Oh! Are you hurt?" She stepped forward, keeping her eyes focused on the writhing heap of hoary animal between them.

"Get back." The command was delivered in a savage, almost inhuman voice.

The great boar struggled to regain its feet, and the man rushed forward to kick it in the head. The beast rooted and snapped with its snout and jaws, trying to bite the man's foot.

One tusk fishhooked on boot leather, pulling the man off balance and sending him crashing to the ground. The two were locked together now, boar's jaw to man's boot, and the stranger used the position to his advantage. Bracing himself on hands and elbows, he stomped and kicked with his free leg, landing vicious blows to the boar's throat, crown, jaw. The boar backed away, dragging the man with him, but the animal couldn't free its tusk. Again and again, the man kicked, until the boar's squeals became choked gurgles. The scent of fresh blood, metallic and sharp, mingled with the beast's own stench.

Cecily backed away, nauseated by the sounds and smells of violence. She tripped over a tree root and stumbled back, coming to rest on her elbows. She stayed like that, staring up at a slice of cloudy sky visible through the branches, until the pummeling blows stopped and the boar wheezed its last rattling breath. Then she slumped back further, laying supine in the leaves. Her heart throbbed against her breastbone.

"Thank you," she whispered to her unknown rescuer. If he hadn't intervened, she would have certainly perished. He must be one of Denny's footmen, she reasoned. Or perhaps a gamekeeper from Swinford or Corbinsdale.

But then, he had no hounds, no gun. Strange.

Feeling sufficiently recovered to risk a look at him, she rolled onto her side.

She saw no one.

A hand clamped around her ankle, and Cecily shrieked. She attempted to rise, but could do no more than scrabble sideways with her leg pinned thus. Her rescuer, now turned attacker, crouched at her feet and began shoving her skirts to her waist. Horrified, she kicked at him the way he'd kicked at the boar, but before her boot could connect with his face, he'd captured it in his other hand. His head disappeared from view, and she felt him burrowing under her petticoats.

Oh, God. What cruel work of Fate was this? This man had preserved her life, only to ravage her body? Temporarily pinning her left leg with his knee, he unlaced and removed her boot. Vise-like fingers gripped the bared arch of her foot.

She shoved at his shoulders through the folds of her skirts, beat on his back with her fists. "No," she sobbed. "No, please."

"Shhh." A rush of hot breath warmed her inner thigh. "Be still," came the rough voice muffled by fabric. "I won't hurt you."

Cecily felt a swift tug at her ribbon garter—and since his hands were occupied restraining her ankles, she knew he had to be using his mouth. She shuddered as the ribbon fell slack and a neat row of teeth closed around the edge of her sensible woolen stocking. Slowly, tenderly, with a lover's finesse, he drew the stocking down her leg. A desperate sensation built within her as the wool scraped over her thigh, her knee, the sensitive slope of her calf. Her senses buzzed with an exquisite blend of heightened awareness and fear. She trembled.

He slid the stocking over her foot, then released both her legs. "Forgive me," he murmured.

Cecily heard him rise to his feet and stride away. She fought to sit up, batting away the folds of cloak and petticoat blocking her view. When she finally managed to get upright, she spied the man retreating into the shadows. His face was impossible to make out. What moonlight remained lit only the pale, tattered remnants of one shirtsleeve and the mud-streaked, sinewy arm beneath. Around his forearm, he had wound her stocking.

A bandage. He had taken her stocking to dress his wound. And it must have been a serious injury, for Cecily could already discern a dark stain of blood seeping through the ivory wool.

"You're wounded." She finally managed to get standing all of a piece, balancing her weight on her right leg as her bare left toes squished in mud. "You need help."

He ignored her, striding away at a purposeful speed. There was no way she could keep pace with him, not missing one boot.

"Stop, please!" she called. "Come back. I know who you are."

And then, the far-off call: "Cecily?"

It was Denny's voice. She cast a quick glance over her shoulder and caught the bobbing glow of torches in the distance.

"Cecily?" he called again. "Is that you? Are you all right?"

She whipped her neck back around to look for the man, but he'd already disappeared. Squinting hard, she scanned the thick curtain of forest, flattening the brown and green shadows into one shapeless mass and hoping for just one stray flash of—

Of quicksilver. There it was. A bolt of mercury, bounding through the trees.

"Cecily!" Denny's voice was now joined by Portia's. "Cecily, where are you?"

"Here," she called. "I'm over here."

The torches moved toward her, and Cecily melted with relief. She'd had enough imprudent adventure for one evening, thank you.

"Cecily. Thank God." Pushing his way into the stand of alder, Denny hurried to her side. He put an arm about her shoulders, and she gratefully leaned into his embrace.

"Where have you been?" Portia scolded. "Why on earth did you leave the group? We've been—"

When a piercing shriek ended her friend's harangue, Cecily knew the torchlight must have illumined the bloody remains of the boar. Not wanting to look, she buried her face in Denny's coat.

"Good Lord," said Brooke. "What's happened here?"

Cecily lifted her face and looked round at the group. Denny, Brooke, all four footmen. It couldn't have been any of them. Her suspicions were confirmed. Dare she tell them the truth?

She swallowed hard. "I've just met the werestag."

Chapter Four

"WELL, THEN." LUKE took his seat at the breakfast table. He was last to arrive, as was his habit, and he addressed his general greetings to the table. "How was your hunting excursion last night? Did you catch a glimpse of your man-beast, Mrs. Yardley?"

"No," Portia replied with a coy smile. "But Cecily did."

He swung his gaze to the other side of the table, where Cecily sat, calmly nipping sugar into her teacup. "Is that so?"

"Yes, it is," she replied in a matter-of-fact tone, not looking up from her tea.

"She caught more than a glimpse of him," Denny said. "And *he* took her boot."

"He did not take my boot. I mean, he took off my boot, but he gave it back. It was my stocking he kept."

"Oh, naturally," Luke muttered.

Cecily gave him a sharp look, clearly annoyed with his flippant response. But really, how *should* he respond to the notion of Cecily disrobing in the woods and distributing items of personal attire to mythical beasts? A servant approached, offering him a plate heaped with eggs and kippers and a ridiculous number of buttered rolls. Rubbing his temples, he waved it away. "Just coffee." Surely this would all make more sense after coffee. "Would someone care to begin this tale at the beginning?"

Cecily looked to Portia. "You're the writer."

Portia lifted her eyebrows. "It's your story."

"I spied a white stag in the forest," Cecily began, carefully buttering a point of toast as she spoke. "I followed him, and became separated from the group. Deep in the woods, a wild boar attacked me. A man appeared from nowhere and killed it."

"Butchered it, more like." Portia shuddered. "What a gruesome scene."

"He saved my life." Cecily's chin lifted. "At great risk to his own. Then he took my stocking to bind his wound and left. Just as I lost sight of the man retreating through the woods, I saw the stag again, bounding away." Her clear blue eyes met Luke's. "It must have been the werestag."

"Absurd," Brooke said. "You didn't see a 'werestag', Miss Hale. You saw a stag, and you saw a man. It does not follow that they are one and the same. The man who came to your aid could have been anyone. A poacher, perhaps. Or a gamekeeper."

"He was unarmed," said Cecily. "He had no hounds."

"Still. There must be some rational explanation. If he was a stag transformed into a man, where did he get clothes? Does he keep them stashed under a bush somewhere?"

Portia asked, "Are you calling Cecily a liar?"

"Not at all," Brooke replied evenly. "But after a traumatic event like that, it would be perfectly understandable if she were confused, overwrought . . ."

"I am not mad," Cecily insisted, letting her butter knife clatter to her plate. "I know what I saw. I am not the sort of hysterical female who imagines things."

"Are you sure?" Luke sipped his coffee. "Are you certain you're not exactly that sort of female? The type to harbor romantic illusions and cling to them for years, hoping they'll one day become the truth?"

Ah, if looks could fillet a man, Luke would have been breakfast. But he would rather have Cecily's anger than her indifference, and for the first time in nine days, that was what he was sensing from her. Whatever, or whoever, she had encountered in the forest—be it man, animal, or something in-between—it had captured her imagination, and her loyalty as well. Those treasures that had so recently, if undeservedly, belonged to him.

Not anymore. The way she defended her tale so stridently, the lively spark in her eyes, the fetching blush staining her throat . . . Luke felt these subtle signals like jabs to his gut.

She was falling out of love with him. And fast.

"I've known Cecily all my life," Denny said from the head of the table. "She's an intelligent woman, both sensible and resourceful. She's also my guest, and I won't have her truthfulness or sanity questioned over breakfast." He propped one forearm on the table and leaned forward, fixing Luke with what was, for ever-affable Denny, a surprisingly stern glare.

Luke acknowledged it with a slight nod. If he must surrender her to this man, it was some solace to see Denny was capable of protecting her. In a breakfast room, at least, if not a cursed forest.

Denny turned to Cecily and laid a hand on her wrist. "If you say you encountered a werestag last night, I believe you. Implicitly."

"Thank you, Denny." She gave him a warm smile.

How sweet. Truly, it made Luke's stomach churn.

Ignoring Brooke's grumbling objection, Luke swiped a roll from his neighbor's plate and chewed it moodily. He ought to be rejoicing, he supposed, or at least feeling relieved. She *should* forget him, she *should* marry Denny, the two of them *should* be disgustingly happy.

But Luke could not be so charitable. For four years, she'd held on to that memory of their first, innocent kiss—and he had too. And he liked believing that no matter what occurred in the future—even if she married Denny, even if an ocean divided them—his and Cecily's thoughts would always wander back to the same place: that graying bench tucked beneath the arbor in Swinford Manor's side garden. He didn't want to believe that she could forget that night. But even now, as she buttered another point of toast, he could sense her mind straying . . . and she wasn't kissing him on a garden bench. She was deep in the forest with a blasted white stag.

Damn it, it wasn't right. When she lay abed at night, she shouldn't see charging boars and violent tussles. She should dream of the scent of night-blooming jasmine and the texture of organdy and the distant strains of an orchestra playing a stately sarabande. As he had, all those freezing, damp nights. As he would, in all the bitter years to come.

What had she called him, last night? An insufferable, arrogant cad. Yes, he was. He wanted Cecily pining for him forever, dreaming she could tame him, yearning for the tender love he could never, ever give. He wanted her to remember the old Luke, not fantasize about some uncivilized beast. And if this "werestag" had eclipsed the memory of their kiss with his gory

39

midnight rescue . . .

Luke just would have to do it one better, and give Cecily a new memory to occupy her thoughts. An experience she could never forget.

DENNY DID NOT play the pianoforte. No one in his household did. Yet when Cecily sat down to the instrument that afternoon, she found it recently polished and tuned to a crisp perfection. He must have had that done for her, in anticipation of her visit. Always so thoughtful, Denny.

Her fingers lingered over the keys, coaxing a somber melody from the instrument.

"Is that my funeral march?" Luke's deep drawl, from somewhere behind her.

She froze to her fingertips.

"Don't stop on my account," he said. "Melancholy does become you so."

She closed her eyes and drew a deep, slow breath. If he wished to taunt her . . . two could play at that game. Her fingers launched into a jaunty folksong, one she knew he would recognize instantly. They'd sung it that summer, practiced it over and over in preparation for that farce of a musicale at Lady Westfall's estate. She played the introduction effortlessly, from memory—not caring that she would betray the fact that she'd practiced it often over the years, out of sentimental folly. And here came the cue for his entrance, that gay little trill that ushered in his bass. She drew the notes out, extending him a musical dare. Would he sing his part? He'd always had the most beautiful voice, before.

"Enough," he said. "I preferred the mournful dirge."

Cecily dropped her hands to her lap. "So it would seem. You are as devoted to low spirits as bottled ones, these days."

"Quite. I think I've developed an aversion to levity. When you marry Denny, together you will be so revoltingly happy, I shall have to remove myself to another county." He came to stand at her shoulder. "Perhaps another continent."

He would leave England again? The thought gutted her. She knew what it was, to fret endlessly about his whereabouts, not even knowing whether he still lived. It was a miserable way to spend one's time.

"I'm not going to marry Denny."

He paused. "You have told him this?"

"Not yet. I will tell him soon."

"When did you decide?"

"Last night." She lifted her face to his and read pure male arrogance in the set of his brow, the little quirk at the corner of his lips. How like him, to think that disastrous kiss had changed everything. "No, not in the drawing room. I knew it later, in the forest."

He clucked his tongue. "Ah, Cecy. Don't tell me you've fallen in love with the werestag? I fear he will make you a prickly husband."

"Don't be absurd. And stop deriding me for my honesty, while you hide behind that ironic smirk."

His eyes hardened, and he set his jaw. Curse him, he still wouldn't let her in.

Exasperated, she pushed back the piano bench and stood. "Of course I do not mean to wed a werestag," she said, crossing to the window. "But that encounter showed me what I truly desire. I want the man who will be there when I need him. The man who will protect me, fight for me."

"I have fought for you, Cecily." His voice was low, and resonant with emotion. "I have fought for you, protected you. I have suffered and bled for you." He approached her, covering the Aubusson carpet with a lithe grace that made her weak in the knees. For a moment, she was reminded of the majestic white stag: the innate pride that forbade him to heed her commands; the sheer, wild beauty of his form. They were so alike, he and Luke.

Cecily's breath caught. What did he mean, he had fought for her, bled for her? Was she referring to last—

"I have fought for you," he repeated, thumping a fist to his chest. "Risked my life on battlefields—for you, and for Denny, and for Brooke and Portia and every last soul who calls England home. Is that not enough?"

Mere inches separated them now. She swayed forward, carving the distance in half. Her heart drummed in her breast as she whispered, "No."

His eyes flared. "Cecy . . ."

"It's not enough." She lifted one hand to his neck, curling her fingers into the velvety hair at his nape. Yes, every bit as soft as it looked. "I want more."

If their game was taunting, victory was hers. Grasping her by the hips, he crushed her to the wall and kissed her with abandon. And unlike a typical kiss, which started with superficial contact and then deepened by degrees, this kiss began at the end. He devoured her in those first desperate seconds, prying her jaw wide, stroking deep with his tongue; but then he soon retreated to gently explore her mouth. And then he was worshipping just her lips—reverently tracing their shape with his tongue, blessing them with feather-soft kisses as she stroked his hair.

Oh. Oh, sweet heaven.

His hands slid up to cup her breasts. She arched against him, pressing her breasts into his palms, thrilling when he thumbed the hardened tips. He bent and kissed her throat, her collarbone, the tender border of her décolletage. His tongue dipped between her breasts, and she clutched him tight.

"Yes," she said aloud, afraid he might stop. This was what she needed. Yes, *yes*.

This was paradise.

HE WOULD MOST certainly go to hell for this.

Luke knew it, and he didn't bloody well care. It was all he could do not to drag her down to the carpet, toss her skirts up around her ears and claim her in the most primitive way possible—what remained of his soul be damned.

He wanted to possess her mouth, her body, her mind and heart. To touch every deep, soft and secret part of her: the tender arch of her palate, the vulnerable curve beneath each breast, the snug corner of her heart where his memory lived.

The mindless wanting surged in his blood, stiffened in his groin, twisted in his chest. It hurt. He ground his hips against hers to soothe the ache, and she shuddered, as though she could glimpse the lewd images cavorting in his mind.

He drew back immediately.

Rein it in.

This wasn't about unleashing his base desires. This was

about giving Cecily a new memory of him, to surpass all others. He'd been her first kiss, all those years ago. For the rest of her life, she would have compared every kiss from every man to that one perfect moment—until he lost control and mauled her last night, erasing that legacy completely.

But there were other firsts he could give her. Other experiences she would remember, measure every other man against. He had to restrain his animal urges, excavate whatever remnants of patience and tenderness still remained to him.

He had to make this very, very good.

She trembled as he eased her neckline downward, freeing the luscious swell of one breast.

"Don't be afraid," he whispered.

"I'm not," she said. Then, pleading: "Just touch me."

Now it was Luke's knees that quivered as he stroked her breast, caressing her with the backs of his fingers before taking the plump weight into his palm. So pale and perfect. So smooth and cool against his tongue. He bent to draw her taut nipple into his mouth, suckling her until he pulled a deep moan from her throat.

With his other hand, he hitched up her skirts. A bit of impatient fumbling—he was out of practice, after all—and he found her sex, warm and dewy with excitement. It nearly undid him, to feel how much she wanted this. Wanted *him*.

Gently, tenderly, he caressed her most sensitive flesh. Learning the shape of her with his fingers, circling her swollen pearl with his thumb. Cecily's breathing quickened, and her eyes fluttered shut.

"Open your eyes," he said. "I want you to know it's me."

She obeyed, looking up at him. "As if it could be anyone

else."

God, the unabashed affection in her gaze . . . It punctured all the defenses he'd built around his heart. A flood of emotions swamped him: anger, confusion, fear. And beneath it all, a foolish, sentimental sort of yearning. He hadn't known he still was capable of yearning, for anything.

She made him feel almost human again.

He sank to his knees, pressing his cheek to the cool silk of her inner thigh. "Cecy, my darling. I could kiss you for that."

And he did.

Spreading his fingers to frame the slit of her drawers, he pressed his mouth to her core. She bucked against him, and he clutched her hips tight, pinning her to the wall as he teased and tasted her flesh. Her gasp of delight made his pulse stutter.

Slowly now. Don't rush.

Yes, he meant to give Cecily an indelible memory, but he was also taking one for himself. He drank in her intoxicating perfume—the scents of clean linen and soap, mingling with the sweet musk of her arousal. He stroked her languidly with his tongue, wanting to memorize her shape, her texture, her taste. Most of all, he took his time learning *her*, delighting in the smallest discoveries: a caress *just so* made her moan; a kiss to *this* spot made her hips convulse.

Be it four years or forty—this would be a kiss to remember.

"*Luke.*"

Her peak came quickly. Too quickly. She gave a startled cry of pleasure and clutched his neck. Shamelessly, he slid a finger inside her, needing to feel that part of her grip him too.

Then it was over. All of it, over.

He caressed her until her breathing slowed. Then, with a

light parting kiss to her thigh, he rearranged her drawers and petticoats before lifting his weight on shaky legs.

What to say, when she looked at him thus? Her heart shining in her eyes, her taste lingering on his tongue. After what they'd just shared, he couldn't lie to her. He couldn't tell her she meant nothing to him, then callously walk away. No, he had to find some way to make her understand she meant everything to him. And while he still must walk away, there would be nothing callous about it.

"Cecy." He smoothed the hair from her face. And then, in a solemn tone of farewell, "You're lovely."

"No." She grasped his lapel with one hand and reached for his trouser falls with the other. "No, don't go." Cupping the hard ridge of his erection, she kissed his neck and whispered fiercely, "I know you want me. You must know I want you too. Luke, I—"

"Don't." Summoning his last shred of restraint, he tugged her hand from the buttons and brought it to his lips. "You may think you want me, but it's Denny you need. You deserve to be happy, Cecily. Adored, doted upon, surrounded by a half-dozen blue-eyed children. I want you to have that life."

"Then give me that life."

"I can't. Don't you see? Everything's different now. I'm different now. I'm not that dashing, immortal youth who kissed you in the garden all those years ago."

She stroked his cheek. "I'm not the giddy, moonstruck girl you kissed. I'm a woman now, with my own fears and desires. And a heart that's grown stronger than you'd credit. Strong enough to contain four years' worth of love."

He cleared his throat and studied the wood paneling. The

whorls of grain twisted and churned as he blinked. "You should have saved it for someone else."

"I've never wanted anyone else." She tugged on his chin until he met her gaze. "*Luke*. Fight for me."

He shook his head. "I'm done with fighting."

"And I'm done with waiting," she said. "If you walk away from me again . . ."

"We're finished. I know." Tenderly, he hooked a wisp of her hair with his fingertip and slowly tucked it behind her ear. "Marry Denny."

She stared at him, lips parted in disbelief. "What a liar you are. You keep insisting you've changed, but you haven't changed one bit. Toying with my affections one moment, callously discarding them the next. I can't decide whether you're deceiving me or just lying to yourself."

"Don't overthink it, Cecy." Turning aside, he tugged casually on each of his cuffs. "You said it best last night. I'm an arrogant, insufferable cad."

He stepped away, stretching the taut thread of silence between them.

Long moments passed before she spoke. "Very well," she said numbly. "I'll speak with Denny today."

"Cecily! Merritt! There you are." Portia burst into the room, clearly too full of excitement to notice Cecily's mussed hair or Luke's skewed cravat, much less the tension hanging in the air. "I've been searching this whole blasted house for you."

Thank God for rambling old estates. If Portia had found them a few minutes earlier . . .

"Come quickly, both of you. Denny's gamekeeper found—" She made an impatient gesture and ran to Cecily's side, taking her arm. "I'll give you the details on the way. We're off to the woods, all of us."

Cecily shot Luke a strange glance before turning to her friend. "What is it, Portia?"

"Why, the werestag, of course."

Chapter Five

"SO YOU'VE DECIDED to join us this time," Denny said.

Luke shrugged. "Didn't want to miss the entertainment."

Together the men covered the sloping green in long, easy strides. Luke glanced over his shoulder at Cecily, who walked between Portia and Brooke. Her pale blue muslin gown caught the late-afternoon breeze, pulling against her soft, feminine curves, and he damn near sighed with longing. Things might be finished between them—they had to be—but he'd be damned if he'd let her wander loose in that forest a second time. The devil only knew what fearsome creature she might meet with, or shed her stocking for, next.

"We're going another way this time," Denny explained. "There's a cottage tucked deep in the forest there." Shading his eyes with one hand, he indicated the direction with the other. "My gamekeeper uses it from time to time, and he found something suspicious there this morning."

"Not suspicious," Portia objected, as the other group joined them at the trailhead. "Gothic and intriguing."

"Please," said Brooke. "A discarded stocking is neither gothic nor intriguing. It's laundry."

Luke's eyes shot to Cecily. "He found the stocking?" He swallowed. "*Your* stocking?"

"So it would seem." She clasped her hands together. "It was . . . soiled."

"Crusted with blood, you mean." Portia's dark eyes widened as she touched Luke's arm. "*Werestag* blood. It's positively chilling. He truly must be the most fearsome, violent sort of creature. I tell you, Lord Merritt, if you could have seen the mincemeat he made of that boar . . ." She shuddered. "No one who witnessed that scene could doubt Cecily's rescuer was half wild beast."

All eyes turned to Cecily. Denny laid a hand on her pale blue sleeve, and Luke felt a possessive fury surge through his veins.

Let it go, he told himself. *Let her go.*

"Portia, he saved my life." Cecily's voice was indignant, and she shrugged off Denny's touch. "Unarmed and unaided, he killed a ferocious boar that would have gored and devoured me. Yes, it was messy. Battles to the death often are. Stop speaking as though he took pleasure in it."

"Your defense is most stirring, Miss Hale." Luke deliberately adopted a formal, detached tone that he knew would only inflame her anger. "You seem to have developed a rather personal attachment to this man-beast."

Tears glittered in her eyes as she glared at him. Tears, and accusations. "He fought for me."

The group fell into an uncomfortable silence. She sniffed and dropped her eyes, and Luke took the opportunity to study her pale expression of distress.

Cecily, Cecily. Foolish girl, to think herself enamored with a beast. She could have no conception of Luke's animal side. There were times during the war he'd been stripped down to it—become a base, feral creature that knew only hunger, sweat and the smells of blood and fear.

She was dreaming after a myth: a gentleman who dallied as a noble beast, rescuing damsels in some enchanted forest. With Luke, she would get a beast wearing the clothes of a man. An uncivilized creature who'd lost all enjoyment in balls and parlor games, who'd forgotten the words to all her trite little songs of green meadows and shepherds and love.

Enjoy your fantasy world, Cecily. Let me visit you there, from time to time.

"Now this is a thrilling development," Portia sang. "I knew it. What an enchanting twist this will make for my novel. The heroine is in love with the werestag."

"No, the heroine is *not*." Fingers pressed to her temples and eyes squeezed shut, Cecily took a deep breath and began again. "Forgive me. But I tell you with perfect candor, I am not in love with a werestag. I'm just feeling . . . a bit out of sorts. Perhaps I've a headache coming on." She extended a hand to Denny. "Will you walk with me? I feel better when you're near."

"But of course." He tucked her hand into the crook of his elbow, and then addressed Luke. "Why don't you lead the others on ahead? The path leads directly to the cottage. It's not as though you could become lost. Cecily and I will catch up."

Luke nodded. He turned and marched forward, a sense of hopelessness hollowing out his chest. He knew exactly what conversation would take place between Cecily and Denny on the way to the cottage. Well. That was that. When they returned to Swinford Manor this evening, he'd instruct his valet to pack up his things. Perhaps Luke would even ride out tonight. He could bring himself to let her go, but he'd be damned if he'd sit around and toast the happy couple's betrothal.

To that, he would drink alone. In copious amounts.

"Very well," said Portia thoughtfully. "Perhaps the heroine is not in love with the werestag. It makes a much better story if the beast is in love with her. So close, and yet so far from his beloved. Doomed to watch her from afar, never to hold her again. How tragically romantic."

"How patently ridiculous," Brooke replied.

Luke strode briskly ahead, leaving them to their quarrel. He would not have admitted it, but he rather agreed with them both.

SHE WOULD TELL him, Cecily bargained with herself, once they reached that small boulder. Or perhaps the little patch of ferns. Failing that, she would most certainly break the news before they passed that gnarled birch tree.

Denny kept pace with her easily, as he always did. Their silence was companionable, as it always was. All the while, Cecily kept up this internal bartering, staving off the inevitable just one more minute . . . and then again one minute more.

At last she halted at a rotted, mossy stump. "I cannot marry you," she told the clump of toadstools flourishing at its base. "I'm so terribly sorry. I should have told you years ago, but—"

"For God's sake, Cecily." His soft laugh startled her, and she lifted her gaze. "You can't do this, not yet. How can a lady refuse a man, when he hasn't even proposed? I won't stand for it."

"It's not right, Denny. I've known for some time now that we wouldn't . . . that I couldn't . . ."

He shushed her gently, placing his hands on her shoulders. "The truth is, we know nothing of what could be or would be. We've been delaying this conversation for years now, haven't we? I've been waiting for . . . Well, I hardly know what I've been waiting for. Something indefinable, I suppose. And you've been waiting for Luke."

Her breath caught. Denny knew? *Oh, dear.* Perhaps she shouldn't be so surprised. They'd grown up together. He'd known her longer than anyone.

"Yes, of course I knew," he said, as if reading her thoughts. "Why do you think I invited you both here, to my home? I wanted to know how matters stood between you."

"And how do they stand?" she asked, hoping he would understand her better than she knew herself.

He sighed. "I know he has some strange hold on your heart. But I believe you'd be happier marrying me."

Cecily shook her head in disbelief. If she didn't know better, she would think him working in concert with Luke. Their arguments were one and the same.

"But, Denny . . ." She prayed these words would not hurt his pride overmuch. "But we don't love one another, not in that way."

"Perhaps not. But you've been in love with Luke for four years now. Has it made you happy?"

She had no answer to that.

"And I'll admit, bachelorhood is losing its charms for me." Gently, he folded her hands in his. "I know there is no grand passion between us, Cecily. But there is genuine caring.

Honesty. Respect. Lasting unions have been built on foundations far weaker than these. And in time, perhaps some deeper attachment would grow. We don't know what could happen, if only we gave it a chance."

He brought her hands to his lips and kissed them warmly—first the knuckles, then each sensitive palm—before pressing them to either side of his face and holding them there. The sweetness in the gesture surprised her, as did the fond regard in his eyes.

This was Denny's face she held in her hands. Dear, familiar, uncomplicated Denny, with the dimple on his right cheek and the tiny pockmark on the other. She'd known this face since her childhood. Could she learn to see to him in a new light, as a husband? She did want children and companionship and a happy home—all the things Luke refused to offer her.

She sighed. "I don't know what to say."

"That's all right. I'm not asking you to say yes, not right now. Just . . . don't say no quite yet?"

He smiled then, that crooked, endearing Denny smile. And he kissed her, still holding her hands pressed against his face.

It was sweet. He tasted of tea and peppermint, and his lips felt soft and warm. Denny's kiss was mild, tender. Comforting and comfortable. And it was wretchedly unfair to him, that even as he claimed her lips, her heart remained divided. She couldn't stop comparing this kiss to Luke's.

It just wasn't the same.

"DO YOU HEAR something?" Portia asked, after they'd been walking some time.

"No," said Brooke.

"Wait!" Portia signaled the men to halt, then put a finger to her lips for silence.

Luke shifted his feet impatiently, anxious to move on. If they stood here too long, Cecily and Denny might catch them.

"There," Portia said, cupping one hand around her ear. "Do you hear it? That rustling sound, like dry leaves."

"Dry leaves, in a forest," Brooke replied. "Imagine."

Luke forged ahead, and the pair followed, bickering in agitated whispers. The cottage couldn't be much farther. Perhaps he could simply barricade the two of them in it and leave. The sooner these two shared a bed, the sooner everyone else could get some peace.

"Wait!" she called again.

Luke pivoted on his heel. "What now?"

"Look at these marks." Portia pointed to a narrow stripe of depressions in the soil. "Why, they look like deer tracks."

Brooke rubbed his eyes. "Deer tracks, in a forest. Imagine."

"But we don't know they belong to a deer! They could belong to him." With a self-conscious hunch of her shoulders, she lowered her voice to a murmur. "You know, the *werestag*."

"Why are you whispering? Afraid the man-deer might overhear you?" Brooke gave a caustic laugh. "My dear Mrs. Yardley, your fancies grow more amusing by the moment. What on earth would lead you to believe these simple deer tracks are the marks of a vicious werestag?"

"I am not *your* 'dear Mrs. Yardley'. And how do you know these tracks do *not* belong to him?"

In a clear expression of annoyance, Brooke held up his hands. "Very well. I give up."

"I don't," she replied, her eyes narrowing. "That is the difference between us." Lifting her skirts, Portia made a quarter turn and stomped directly off into the woods.

"Just where do you think you're going?"

"I'm following the tracks, of course. That's the only way to learn the truth."

As Portia's dark cloak disappeared into the trees, Luke started after her. A wave of dread swamped his progress. "Mrs. Yardley, wait," he called. "It's unsafe to go walking off the path. At least let me—"

A metallic snap cut him off.

Followed by a piercing scream.

Luke and Brooke charged through the foliage. They found Portia lying sprawled in leaves and moss, her face gone utterly white.

"My . . . " She gulped for air. "Help me. I don't know what's happened to my foot."

With shaking fingers, she drew her skirts up to the ankles. The steel jaws of a trap held her left boot clenched in their deadly bite.

"Bloody hell." Brooke sank to his knees at her side. "Don't worry, Portia. We'll have it off straightaway." He reached for the trap.

"Wait," Luke said. "Don't—"

Another tortured scream from Portia.

"Touch it," he finished weakly.

"What's happened?" Cecily and Denny joined them, linked arm in arm as they pushed through the brush.

"She's stepped in a trap," Luke replied, not risking a glance at Cecily's face. "A small one, fortunately, but it has quite a grip on her foot. We'll have to pry it off." He scouted around him for a suitable branch, pausing only long enough to catch Denny's eye. "Find me two sturdy poles, about six feet in length. I can release her from the trap, but we'll need a pallet to carry her home."

Denny nodded, and with a murmured word to Cecily, began searching the environs for saplings.

"It hurts," Portia moaned. "It hurts so much. I must be dying."

"Of course you aren't." Folding her skirts, Cecily settled at her friend's side. Luke could feel her blue eyes on him as he selected a thick branch and stripped it of twigs.

Having removed his coat, Brooke folded it and propped it beneath Portia's head, for a pillow. "You can't die," he told her, crouching at her other side. "Who would argue with me then?"

"Anyone with sense," she said tartly. But when Brooke took her hand, Portia allowed him to keep it. "Don't you aggravating know-all's have some sort of debating society?"

"Yes, but none of the members have your amusing imagination. Nor such lovely hair." He stroked an ebony lock from her pale, sweating brow.

Luke pushed her skirts to the knee and took a firm grip on his branch. "Mrs. Yardley, this is going to hurt."

Portia whimpered.

Brooke kept stroking her hair, murmuring, "Be brave, darling. Scream all you like. Break every bone in my hand, if you must. I won't leave your side."

Cecily moved toward Luke. "How can I help?"

"You can't."

"I can," she insisted. "Just tell me what to do. Shall I help you pry?"

"No," he replied tersely. Damn it, he didn't want to expose Cecily to this, but an extra pair of hands would be useful. "Just . . . hold her. Keep her ankle steady, even if she bucks."

She nodded. "Portia, I'm going to hold your leg now." Her delicate fingers closed around her friend's ankle and calf, in grips so tight her knuckles blanched. "I'm ready."

He bent his head and threaded the branch between the jaws of the trap. Despite his attempt not to jostle Portia's leg, he could not help but brush it. Her low moan of pain was met with more murmured assurances from Brooke.

Luke looked to Cecily, anxious to gauge her reaction.

"Go ahead," she said calmly, still gripping Portia's leg. "Just do it."

Luke braced his boot and levered the branch with all his strength. Pain ripped through his forearm, and Portia released a bloodcurdling scream that surely belonged in one of her gothic novels. But Cecily held her friend's leg stoically, using all her weight to keep it still.

Within a few seconds, Luke had pried the jaws apart. "Now," he commanded in a grunt, and Cecily understood him. She pulled her friend's boot up and out of the trap, a half second before the branch splintered and the metal spikes snapped on air.

"We'll need to assess her wound," Cecily said, unlacing her friend's boot while Luke stood panting for breath. She had Portia's boot and shredded stocking removed within seconds.

Together they knelt over her wounded foot.

"These don't look deep," Luke said, observing the two puncture wounds on Portia's pale foot. "And only a scratch below."

"Thank heaven for sensible shoes." Cecily flashed him a little smile.

A sweet pang of affection caught him in the chest. She was handling this so well, soothing everyone—Luke included—with her serene competence and dry humor. Where had she learned how to cope with scenes like this? Certainly not in finishing school.

Desperate to distract himself before he lost sight of any goal but kissing her, Luke returned his gaze to the wound. After studying it a few moments more, he said, "It'll need to be cleansed thoroughly. But we'd best bind it for now, until we can get her back to the Manor. Cecy, give me your—"

"Stocking?" A wide ribbon of ivory flannel dangled before his eyes.

He looked up, startled. Her expression was all innocence.

"I was going to say handkerchief," he lied, taking the garment from her. "But this will do."

As Cecily jammed her bare foot back into her boot, Luke looped the stocking over Portia's foot and ankle repeatedly, binding her wounds tight.

Denny returned, two serviceable poles in hand. Luke stripped off his own coat and threaded a pole through either sleeve before buttoning it down the middle. He did the same with Brooke's coat, coming from the poles' opposite end. The result was a makeshift conveyance that would bear Portia's weight easily.

Brooke fussed over the wounded lady as they transferred her to the pallet, going so far as to plant a kiss on her brow to praise her bravery.

"What a kiss," Portia complained. "As if I were a child."

Brooke cupped her face in his hands and kissed her thoroughly. He released her only when Portia's faint growl of protest melted to a pleased sigh. "There, was that better?"

"Quite." Portia's cheeks pinked.

"All right, then. Now be a good little girl, and lie still."

She swatted at him feebly as he and Denny lifted the pallet—Brooke carrying the end at Portia's head, and Denny lifting her feet.

Cecily went to Denny's side. "I . . . I must rest a moment, but Portia needs a doctor's attention. Please go ahead with her. Luke will see me home." She popped up on her tiptoes to reward Denny's nod of agreement with a light kiss to his cheek.

As if he were a child, Luke thought pettily.

And then somehow, they were alone.

"Will you walk with me?" she asked, suddenly standing at his elbow.

He silently offered his arm, but she shook her head, reaching for his hand instead.

Fingers laced in that intimate, innocent clasp favored by children and lovers alike, they covered the short distance back to the path.

"Not that way," she said, when he turned to follow the others. "Let's continue on to the cottage. We've come this far, and I may as well retrieve my stocking. I seem to find myself missing another."

"As you wish."

They walked on, their linked hands dangling and swinging between them. And it all felt so easy, so comfortable—as if they were on one of their leisurely strolls that summer four years past.

Of course, they had conversed during those walks. Talked of everything and nothing, in the way courting couples do. When had he lost his ability to make simple conversation? Surely Luke could find it within himself to say *something*.

"You are remarkable," he blurted out, because it was the only thought in his head. "The way you responded to Portia's injury, without fear or hesitation . . . I didn't know you had it in you."

"What, bravery? I didn't always know I had it in me, either. But I do." She gave him a pointed look. "I'd imagine we've each discovered new sides of ourselves in the past four years."

All too true. But the discoveries Luke had made, he would never share with her. Shrugging defensively, he deflected her silent question. "You used to bolt at the sight of a spider."

"Oh, I still hate spiders. But injuries do not frighten me. When a lady spends a year tending invalid soldiers, she sees sights far worse than Portia's wound."

Luke stopped in his tracks, pulling her to a halt as well. "You spent a year nursing invalid soldiers?"

She nodded. "At the Royal Hospital in Chelsea."

"But . . ." He struggled to bend his mind around the idea. "But they don't allow random gentlewomen to nurse invalid soldiers. Do they?"

"Well . . ." She shrugged and resumed walking. "I never precisely asked permission. You see, over a year ago there was a tragic case. A wounded soldier was found wandering near Ardennes. Evidently he was the sole survivor of his regiment. But he'd sustained a severe blow to the head, and he had no memory of who he was, or his home or family or anything before the battle. The papers printed articles about the 'Lost

Hero of Montmirail'. He was the talk of London, and Portia was desperate to go visit him. She had this vain hope that he might be Yardley—she'd just received notice of his death in France, you see, and wanted to believe there'd been some mistake. And I . . ." Slowing, she looked up at Luke. "I wanted to be sure he wasn't you."

A lump formed in his throat.

"But of course he wasn't you," she went on, "nor Yardley. While we were waiting to see him, I found myself talking with another man. A naval officer, wounded in a Danish gunboat attack. He called me in from the corridor, then apologized when he saw my face. He'd mistaken me for his sister."

Cecily sniffed and continued, "Well, I felt terrible for disappointing him, so I stayed with him for an hour or so, just talking. Mostly listening. And then the next day, I came back, and sat with him again. He introduced me to a fellow patient, this one a lieutenant in the cavalry. I don't recall deciding to make it a habit. Day after day, I just kept returning to the hospital. For the first month or so, I did no more than I had the first day—I would simply sit at a patient's bedside and listen. Perhaps read aloud, if he liked. But then, sometimes it was impossible not to notice that their wounds needed tending, bandages needed replacing, and so forth. So I did those small things too."

Luke could only stare at her. Yes, it was true. Cecily *had* changed. Her youthful sweetness and generosity had not disappeared, but added to them now were a woman's serenity and confidence. One could see it in the tilt of her chin, the efficient grace of her movements. And the way the light glowed through the curling wisps of hair at her brow . . . She'd always been a pretty girl, but he'd never thought her so beautiful as he did this very moment.

"Remarkable," he murmured. Clearing his throat, he added, "You didn't find it tedious, listening to all those ragged soldiers rattle on? It didn't repulse you, tending the wounds of complete strangers?"

"Not at all," she answered lightly, squeezing his hand. "I just pretended they were you."

God. She was killing him.

"Well then," he said in a tone of false nonchalance, "I'm certain every last one of them fell hopelessly in love with you. How many proposals have you rejected in the past four years? A hundred or more, I'm sure."

"Twenty-six."

Luke slowed as the cottage came into view—a tidy, thatched-roof dwelling hunched between two tall pine trees.

"Twenty-six," he repeated, coming to a stop.

She turned to him, clutching his hand tight. "Yes. Twenty-six. Not counting the invalid soldiers." The color of her eyes deepened to an intense cobalt blue. "You cannot know how I have fought for you, Luke. Not in the same way you have suffered, to be sure. But I have waged my own small battles here. I have fought the pressure to marry, fought the envy for my friends who did. I have struggled against my own desire for companionship and affection." Her voice broke. "I am not a woman formed for solitude."

"I know it," he whispered, raising his free hand to her cheek. "I know it. That's why you need a husband who can—"

"I have fought despair," she interrupted, "when months, *years* passed with no word of you."

Guilt twisted in his gut. "I could not have written. We weren't engaged."

"Yes, but you might have written Denny. Or any one of our mutual friends. You might have casually asked for word of me."

"I didn't want word of you."

She recoiled, and he whipped an arm around her waist, pulling her close.

"How can I explain? You know my parents died several years ago. I've no siblings, very few relations. And it didn't take but one dusty skirmish in Portugal for me to realize—if I died on that battlefield, there would be no one to mourn me, but a handful of old school friends." He touched her cheek. "No one but you. I did think of you. Constantly. I did remember that perfect, sweet kiss when I was bleeding and starving and pissing scared. It was the thought that kept me going: Cecily Hale cares whether I live or die. I couldn't risk asking word of you, don't you understand? I didn't want to know. Surely I'd learn you'd married one of those twenty-six men queuing up for the pleasure of your hand, and I would have nothing left."

"But I didn't marry any of them. I waited for you."

"Then you were a fool." He gripped her chin. "Because that man you waited for . . . he isn't coming back. I've changed, too much. Some men lose a leg in war; others, a few fingers. I surrendered part of my humanity. Just like the ridiculous werestag you're out here chasing."

"I'm out here chasing you, you idiot!" She buffeted his shoulder with her fist. "You're the one I love."

He kissed her, hard and fast. Just for a moment. Just until her mouth stopped forming dangerous words and melted to a soft, generous invitation, and her fisted hand uncurled against his chest.

Then he pulled away.

"Listen to me. I admire you. Adore you. Hell, I've spent four years constructing some twisted, blasphemous religion around you. And you must know how badly I want you." He slid a hand to the small of her back and crushed her belly against his aching groin, then kissed her again, to stifle his unwilling groan. "But I can't love you, Cecily, not the way you deserve."

"Who are you, to judge what I deserve?" She wrestled away from him and stalked to the cottage door, taking hold of the door handle and giving it a full-force tug. "And what do you mean, you *can't* love me? Love isn't a matter of can or can't." She pulled again, but the door would not budge. "It's a matter of do or don't. Either you do love me, and damn the consequences"—she tugged again, to no avail—"or you don't, and we go our separate ways."

She let go the door handle and released an exasperated huff.

Slowly, he walked to her side. "There's a little latch," he said, pulling on the string above her head. "Just here."

The door swung open with a rusty creak. Together they stood on the threshold, peering into the cottage's dimly lit interior.

"After you," Cecily said wryly. "By all means."

"The light's fading. We should return to the manor."

"Not yet," she said, pushing him forward into the dirt-floored gloom. "Strip off your shirt."

Chapter Six

"WHAT?" LUKE CROSSED his arms over his chest. His eyes darted from the cottage's single window to the straw-tick bed huddled under the sloping corner of the roof. "You can't be serious."

Cecily found his panic vastly amusing. "Certainly I can."

"Cecy, this is hardly the time and place for—"

"A tryst?" She laughed. "You think I mean to trap you in this secluded cottage and have my wicked way with you? You should be so lucky. No, remove your shirt. I want a look at your arm."

"My arm?" His eyes narrowed. "Which one?"

"Which one do you think?" She crossed to him and began unknotting the cravat at his neck. "The one you injured while wrestling the boar last night."

Oh, the look on his face . . .

Cecily wanted to kiss him. He was so adorably befuddled. At last, he'd let slip that hard mask of indifference he'd been wearing since his arrival at Swinford Manor. And in its place— there was *Luke*. Engaging green eyes, touchable dark brown hair, those lips so perfectly formed for roguish smiles and tender kisses alike.

This was the man she'd fallen in love with. The man she still loved now. Yes, he'd changed, but she had too. She was older, wiser, stronger than the girl she'd been. This time, she wouldn't let him go.

"You knew?"

She smiled. "I knew."

His breath hitched as she slipped the cravat from his neck. Attempting to ignore the wedge of bare chest it revealed, and the mad pounding of her blood that view inspired, Cecily set to work on his waistcoat buttons.

"How?" he asked, obeying her silent urgings to shed the garment. "How did you know?"

"It's a fortunate thing you weren't assigned to espionage. You've no talent for disguise whatsoever. If I hadn't suspected already, I would have figured it out this afternoon. My stocking was found in this remote cottage, and you just happen to know the secrets of the door latch? Then there's the fact that you've been favoring your arm since breakfast." She undid the small closure of his shirtfront before turning her attention to his cuffs. "But I knew you last night. I'd know your voice anywhere, not to mention your touch." She gave a shaky sigh, unable to meet his questioning gaze. "It's like you said, Luke. You still make me tremble, even after all these years."

His voice was soft. "I don't even know why I followed you. The way we'd parted so angrily . . . I just couldn't let you go, not like that."

"And I'm glad of it. You saved my life." With a brisk snap, she jerked the shirt's hem from the waistband of his trousers, gathering the fine linen in both hands. "Arms up, head down."

She made a move to lift the shirt over his head, but he

stopped her.

"I caught a bayonet at Vitoria. I've scars. They're not pretty."

"I've been tending wounded soldiers for a year. I'm certain I've seen worse."

And she *had* seen worse, Cecily reminded herself as she surveyed the pink, rippling scar slanting from his collarbone to his ribs. She had seen worse, but not on anyone she loved. It was so difficult to contain all the silly feminine impulses welling up inside her: the desire to weep, to hold and rock him, to trace his scar with her lips.

But he wouldn't want that sort of fuss.

Clearing her throat, she turned her attention to his injured forearm. It was a clean wound, and not deep enough to be truly worrisome. But as she'd suspected, the binding had come loose—most likely when he'd sprung Portia's trap.

"There's water," he said, nodding toward a covered basin on the table. "I filled it last night."

Together they moved toward the table and settled on the two rough-hewn stools. Cecily dipped her handkerchief in the cool liquid, then dabbed his arm with it.

"If you knew last night," he asked quietly, "why tell the others it was a werestag?"

"Because it was obvious you didn't want the others to know."

"Hang the others. I didn't want *you* to know." He swallowed hard, and stared into the corner. "I never wanted you to see me like that. When a man faces death, he meets the animal lurking inside him. When it's hand to hand, blade to blade, kill or be killed . . ." Defiant green eyes met hers, and he slapped a hand to his scar. "The man who did this to me—I killed him. With his bayonet stuck in my flesh, I reached out and grabbed him by the throat and watched his eyes bulge from his skull as he suffocated at my hand."

She would not react, Cecily told herself, calmly dabbing at his wound. That's what he expected, what he feared—her reaction of revulsion or disgust.

"And he wasn't the only one," he continued. "To learn what violence you're truly capable of, in those moments . . . It's a burden I'd not wish on anyone."

She risked a glance at him then. "Burdens are lighter when they're shared."

Luke swore. "I've shared too much of it with you already. I can't believe I'm telling you this."

"You can tell me anything. I'll still love you. And I warn you, I've learned something of tenacity in the past four years. I'm not going to let you go."

He shook his head. "You don't understand. Sometimes, I scarcely feel human anymore. The brutal way I took down that boar, Cecily. That barbarism with the stocking . . ."

"Ah, yes." She put aside her handkerchief and stood. "The stocking."

She propped one boot on the stool and slowly rucked up her skirts to reveal her stocking-clad leg.

"Cecy . . ."

"Yes, Luke?" She leaned over to untie the laces of her boot, giving him an eyeful of her décolletage.

He groaned. "Cecy, what are you doing?"

"Tending to your wounds," she said, slipping the boot from her foot. With sure fingers, she unknotted the ribbon garter at her thigh, then eased the stocking down her leg. "Making it better." Skirts still hiked thigh-high, she straddled his legs and nestled on his lap.

"Shh." She quieted his objection, then deftly wound the length of flannel around his injured arm, tucking in the end to secure it. "There," she said in a husky voice, lowering her lips to the underside of his wrist. "All better."

"I wasn't after your damn stocking," he blurted out. "When I took you to the ground last night and pushed up your skirts. By all that's holy, I wanted—" With a muttered oath, he gripped her by the shoulders, hauling her further into his lap. Until she felt the hard ridge of his arousal, pressing insistently against her cleft. "Cecily, what I want from you is not tender. It's not romantic in the least. It's plunder. It's possession. If you had the least bit of sense, you'd turn and run from—"

She kissed him hard, raking his back with her fingernails and clutching his thighs between hers like a vise. Boldly, she sucked his lower lip into her mouth and gave it a sharp nip, savoring his startled moan. Wriggling backward, she placed her hands over his, dragging them downward and molding his fingers around her breasts. "For God's sake, Luke. You're not the only one with animal urges."

He took her mouth, growling against her lips as he did. Tongues tangled; teeth clashed. With a small rip of fabric, he liberated her breasts from her stays and bodice, fastening his lips over one pert, straining nipple. He licked roughly, even caught the tender nub in his teeth, and Cecily gasped with shock and delight.

Then his hand left her breast and strayed downward, tunneling through the layers of skirts and petticoats and drawers to find her most intimate flesh. He stroked her there, so tenderly. Too tenderly.

Impatient with desire, she grasped his shoulders and rocked against his hand. A thrill of exquisite anticipation coursed down to her toes. She licked his ear and heard his answering moan.

Yes. *Yes.* This was finally going to happen.

"God," he choked out. "This can't happen."

"Oh, yes it can." Breathless, she worked the buttons of his trouser falls. "It will. It must." Having freed the closures of his trousers and smallclothes, she snaked her hand through the opening and brazenly took him in hand.

Of course, now that she had him in hand, she wasn't quite sure what to do with him. She tentatively skimmed one fingertip over the smooth, rounded crown of his erection. In return, he pressed a single finger into her aching core.

"Cecily." He shut his eyes and grit his teeth. "If I don't stop this now . . ."

"You never will?" She pressed her lips to his earlobe. "That's my fondest hope. You say you're done with fighting, Luke? Then stop fighting this."

He sighed deep in his chest, and she felt all the tension coiled in those powerful muscles release. "Very well," he said quietly, resting his chin on her shoulder. "Very well. To you, I gratefully surrender."

Clutching her bottom with both hands, he rose to his feet, startling a little shriek from her.

"Too late for protests," he teased, carrying her toward the cottage's narrow bed and tossing her onto it. With an impressive economy of movement, he stripped himself of his boots, trousers and smallclothes before settling his weight onto the bed. "Now you."

All that remained of the daylight was a faint, dusky glow filtering through the small window and the chinks in the thatching overhead. He helped her out of her gown and petticoats, then loosened her stays and the ribbon tie of her drawers. When she was completely bared, he sat back on his haunches and regarded her with a quiet intensity. He sat that way for so long, she began to grow anxious.

"Luke? Is everything—"

"Promise me," he said hoarsely, "that you will give me another opportunity to do this properly." Shaky fingertips traced the pale curve of her hip. "You are so beautiful, Cecily. Yours is a body that deserves to be worshipped, adored. Promise me the chance to kiss every lovely, perfect inch of you—next time."

How she loved those words, *next time*. She nodded as he prowled up her body. "Of course."

"Good." His voice was strained as he lowered his weight onto hers. "Because—forgive me, darling—this time will have to be quick."

She gasped as he insinuated one hand between them, probing the slick folds of her sex and spreading her thighs apart. Then she felt the blunt head of him—*there*—pressing, pushing, stretching her to the point of pain. And beyond.

"Are you hurt?" He panted against her neck.

"A little."

"Shall I stop?"

"No." She clutched his back and hooked her legs over his. "Don't you dare." She had fought for him, fought to experience this pain, and she felt oddly possessive of the dull ache between her legs. She wouldn't let him take it away. The pain was real, it was *now*—it meant he had truly come home at last. Home to her.

All too soon, the ache dissipated, lessening with each thrust, and a desperate yearning took its place. She rose up to meet each wild buck of his hips, her hands sliding over his back on a thin sheen of perspiration. His tempo increased, driving her closer and closer to that horizon of delicious pleasure he'd pushed her beyond that afternoon. But this time, it would be so much better. This time he would come too.

With a guttural moan, he froze deep inside her. His gaze caught hers, and Cecily instinctively understood the question in his eyes. They could create a child this way, if she allowed him to continue.

She swept a lock of hair from his brow and waited. He knew her feelings already. This decision should be his.

"I do," he said roughly. "My God, Cecily. I do love you."

Joy swelled inside her, until she trembled with the effort of containing it. Smiling up at him, she whispered, "Then damn the consequences."

No more words after that. Only sighs and moans and wild, inarticulate urgings. *Faster. More. There. Yes, there.*

Now.

"CAN WE STAY here all night?" Cecily asked. She lay tangled with him on the narrow bed, struggling to catch her breath. Only now growing aware of the musty closeness in the cottage.

"We could," he answered sleepily. "If we wish to be awoken by Denny's footmen crashing down the door. He'll have them all searching for us soon enough."

"He knows I'm with you." *In more ways than one.* She felt a pang of sympathy for her old friend. There'd been true disappointment in his expression, when she'd broken their kiss and refused him that afternoon. But Denny deserved to find love too, and she never could have made him truly happy. Not when her heart and soul belonged to Luke.

As if exerting his claim on her body as well, Luke tightened his arms around her. Kissing the hollow of her throat, he murmured, "Perhaps we can stay a half hour more."

Afterward, they rose and dressed quietly, pausing to tidy the small dwelling before latching the door as they left. The night was cloudless, and the nearly full moon provided them sufficient light to follow the path. They walked hand in hand.

"Did you see it last night?" she asked quietly. "The stag?"

"Yes."

"It was beautiful." When he didn't answer, she added, "Don't you agree?" Perhaps men did not think animals "beautiful", or did not admit to it if they did.

"Yes." He gave her a rare, easy smile. "It reminded me of you. Beautiful, graceful, fearless."

"And here I thought him so much like you. Proud, wild, strong." She laughed softly. "Perhaps he didn't exist at all, and we were just out here chasing each other."

If the stag truly existed, they did not see it again before reaching the border of Swinford Woods and emerging onto the green. Then again, a whole herd of bloodthirsty man-deer could have been lurking in the thickets, and Cecily would have remained oblivious. She only had eyes for Luke.

And that fact must have been painfully obvious to Denny, when he nearly collided with them at the entrance to the drawing room.

"Cecily." His gaze wandered from her unbound hair to her disheveled gown, to her fingers still laced with Luke's. "I . . . I was just about to go searching for you."

"There you are!" Portia called from behind him. "Come in, come in." She lay swaddled in blankets on the divan, with her bandaged leg propped on a nearby ottoman. Brooke sat beside her, balancing a teacup in either hand.

Cecily turned to Denny. "I'm sorry to have worried you, but . . ." She squeezed Luke's hand for courage. "You see, Luke and I—"

"I understand," he replied. The serious expression on his face told her he did understand, completely. To his credit, he took it well. He turned to Luke. "When will you be married?"

"Married?" Portia exclaimed.

Cecily sighed. Just like Denny, to take his responsibilities as her third cousin twice removed—and only male relation in the vicinity—so seriously. But did he have to force the issue now? Certainly, she hoped that she and Luke might one day—

"As soon as possible." Luke's arm slid around her waist.

Cecily's gaze snapped up to his. *Are you certain?* she asked him silently.

He answered her with a quick kiss.

"Well, then. When can *we* be married?" Brooke directed his question to Portia.

"Married!" Blushing furiously, Portia made a dismissive gesture with both hands. "Why, I'm only just learning to enjoy being a widow. I don't want to be married. I want to write scandalous novels and take dozens of lovers."

Brooke raised an eyebrow. "Can that be negotiated to lov*er*, singular?"

"That," she said, giving him a coy smile, "would depend on your skill at negotiation."

"What an evening you've had, Portia," Cecily said. "A brush with death, a proposal of marriage, an indecent proposition . . . Surely you have sufficient inspiration for your gothic novel?"

"Too much inspiration!" Portia wailed, gesturing toward her bandaged foot. "I am done with gothics completely. No, I shall take a cue from my insipid wallpaper and write a bawdy little tale about a wanton dairymaid and her many lovers."

"Lover, singular." Brooke flopped on the divan and settled her feet in his lap.

"Oh," she sighed, as he massaged her uninjured foot. "Oh, very well."

Luke tugged on Cecily's hand, drawing her toward the doorway. "Let's make our escape."

As they left, she heard Denny say in his usual jocular tone, "Do me a favor, Portia? Model your hero after me. Just once, I should like to get the girl."

Cecily and Luke tumbled into the corridor, hands still linked.

"I'm sorry," he said, twirling her to a stop and backing her against the wall. "I didn't have a chance to ask for your hand properly, but . . . you don't have an objection, do you?"

She paused a moment to savor the endearing vulnerability in his expression. Then she kissed him soundly, threading her fingers into his hair and pressing her body to his. "There," she said finally. "Does that feel like an objection?"

He smiled and planted a light kiss between her eyebrows before resting his forehead against hers. Between them, their hands made a tight knot of fingers and thumbs.

"I'll leave within the hour," he said, "to go speak with your father. I cannot expect even Denny to be so generous as to continue hosting his rival in this house. And I couldn't spend another night here without having you in my bed."

"As if I would find that objectionable."

They kissed again, and he pressed her against the wall, his hips grinding deliciously against hers. "We must have"—*kiss*—"a very brief"—*kiss*—"engagement."

"Can we not just elope? I could pack a valise in a trice."

He laughed softly into her hair, and she thought it the most beautiful sound in the world.

"Cecy," he whispered against her ear, "tell me this is not a dream. Are you truly mine at last?"

"Oh, Luke." She slid her arms about his waist and gripped him tight. "I always have been."

Thanks for reading!

I hope you enjoyed *How to Catch a Wild Viscount!*

If you'd like to learn more about me or my books, please visit www.TessaDare.com, or sign up for my e-mail newsletter (tessadare.com/newsletter-signup/) to be notified whenever I have a new release. You can also follow me on Twitter at @tessadare, or like my Facebook page at http://facebook.com/tessadareauthor.

If you're new to my books and wondering what to read next, I suggest starting with my bestselling Spindle Cove series. I had great fun creating a seaside village populated by young women who defied the conventions of their time—engaging in such unladylike pursuits as medicine, geology, and artillery. And I had even more fun dreaming up the strong-willed, unsuspecting men who found their hearts ensnared by these unlikely heroines.

Turn the page for an excerpt from Spindle Cove book one, *A Night to Surrender*.

A Night to Surrender: Excerpt

"Lively and sexy, this funny, enjoyable battle of the sexes ensnares readers in a delightful adventure."

- Library Journal

Spindle Cove is the destination of choice for certain types of well-bred young ladies: the awkward, the delicate, the painfully shy; young wives disenchanted with matrimony and young girls *too* enchanted with the wrong men. It's a haven for the women who live there.

Victor Bramwell, the new Earl of Rycliff, knows he doesn't belong in "Spinster Cove," but he has orders to gather a militia. It's a simple mission, made complicated by the spirited, exquisite Susanna Finch—a woman who is determined to save her personal utopia from the invasion of Bram's makeshift army.

The scene is set for an epic battle . . . but who can be named the winner when both have so much to lose?

Sussex, England
Summer 1813

BRAM STARED INTO a pair of wide, dark eyes. Eyes that reflected a surprising glimmer of intelligence. This might be the rare female a man could reason with.

"Now, then," he said. "We can do this the easy way, or we

can make things difficult."

With a soft snort, she turned her head. It was as if he'd ceased to exist.

Bram shifted his weight to his good leg, feeling the stab to his pride. He was a lieutenant colonel in the British Army, and at over six feet tall, he was said to cut an imposing figure. Typically, a pointed glance from his quarter would quell the slightest hint of disobedience. He was not accustomed to being ignored.

"Listen sharp, now." He gave her ear a rough tweak and sank his voice to a low threat. "If you know what's good for you, you'll do as I say."

Though she spoke not a word, her reply was clear: *You can kiss my great woolly arse.*

Confounded sheep.

"Ah, the English countryside. So charming. So . . . fra-grant." Colin approached, stripped of his London-best topcoat, wading hip-deep through the river of wool. Blotting the sheen of perspiration from his brow with a handkerchief, he asked, "I don't suppose this means we can simply turn back?"

Ahead of them, a boy pushing a handcart had overturned his cargo, strewing corn all over the road. It was an open buffet, and every ram and ewe in Sussex appeared to have answered the invitation. A vast throng of sheep bustled and bleated around the unfortunate youth, gorging themselves on the spilled grain—and completely obstructing Bram's wagons.

"Can we walk the teams in reverse?" Colin asked. "Perhaps we can go around, find another road."

Bram gestured at the surrounding landscape. "There is no other road."

They stood in the middle of the rutted dirt lane, which occupied a kind of narrow, winding valley. A steep bank of gorse rose up on one side, and on the other, some dozen yards of heath separated the road from dramatic bluffs. And below those—*far* below those—lay the sparkling turquoise sea. If the air was seasonally dry and clear, and Bram squinted hard at that thin indigo line of the horizon, he might even glimpse the northern coast of France.

So close. He'd get there. Not today, but soon. He had a task to accomplish here, and the sooner he completed it, the sooner he could rejoin his regiment. He wasn't stopping for anything.

Except sheep. Blast it. It would seem they were stopping for sheep.

A rough voice said, "I'll take care of them."

Thorne joined their group. Bram flicked his gaze to the side and spied his hulking mountain of a corporal shouldering a flintlock rifle.

"We can't simply shoot them, Thorne."

Obedient as ever, Thorne lowered his gun. "Then I've a cutlass. Just sharpened the blade last night."

"We can't butcher them, either."

Thorne shrugged. "I'm hungry."

Yes, that was Thorne—straightforward, practical. Ruthless.

"We're all hungry." Bram's stomach rumbled in support of the statement. "But clearing the way is our aim at the moment, and a dead sheep's harder to move than a live one. We'll just have to nudge them along."

Thorne lowered the hammer of his rifle, disarming it, then flipped the weapon with an agile motion and rammed the butt end against a woolly flank. "Move on, you bleeding beast."

The animal lumbered uphill a few steps, prodding its neighbors to scuttle along in turn. Downhill, the drivers urged the teams forward before resetting their brakes, unwilling to surrender even those hard-fought inches of progress.

The two wagons held a bounty of supplies to refit Bram's regiment: muskets, shot, shells, wool and pipeclay for uniforms. He'd spared no expense, and he *would* see them up this hill. Even if it took all day, and red-hot pain screamed from his thigh to his shinbone with every pace. His superiors thought he wasn't healed enough to resume field command? He would prove them wrong. One step at a time.

"This is absurd," Colin grumbled. "At this rate, we'll arrive next Tuesday."

"Stop talking. Start moving." Bram nudged a sheep with his boot, wincing as he did. With his leg already killing him, the last thing he needed was a pain in the arse, but that's exactly what he'd inherited, along with all his father's accounts and possessions: responsibility for his wastrel cousin, Colin Sandhurst, Lord Payne.

He swatted at another sheep's flank, earning himself an indignant bleat and a few inches more.

"I have an idea," Colin said.

Bram grunted, unsurprised. As men, he and Colin were little more than strangers. But during the few years they'd overlapped at Eton, his younger cousin had been just full of ideas. Ideas that had landed him shin-deep in excrement. Literally, on at least one occasion.

Colin looked from Bram to Thorne and back again, eyes keen. "I ask you, gentlemen. Are we, or are we not, in possession of a great quantity of black powder?"

"Tranquility is the soul of our community."

Not a quarter mile's distance away, Susanna Finch sat in the lace-curtained parlor of the Queen's Ruby, a rooming house for gently bred young ladies. With her were the rooming house's newest prospective residents, a Mrs. Highwood and her three unmarried daughters.

"Here in Spindle Cove, young ladies enjoy a wholesome, improving atmosphere." Susanna indicated a knot of ladies clustered by the hearth, industriously engaged in needlework. "See? The picture of good health and genteel refinement."

In unison, the young ladies looked up from their work and smiled placid, demure smiles.

Excellent. She gave them an approving nod.

Ordinarily, the ladies of Spindle Cove would never waste such a beautiful afternoon stitching indoors. They would be rambling the countryside, or sea-bathing in the cove, or climbing the bluffs. But on days like these, when new visitors came to the village, everyone understood some pretense at propriety was necessary. Susanna was not above a little harmless deceit when it came to saving a young woman's life.

"Will you take more tea?" she asked, accepting a fresh pot from Mrs. Nichols, the inn's aging proprietress. If Mrs. Highwood examined the young ladies too closely, she might notice that mild Gaelic obscenities occupied the center of Kate Taylor's sampler. Or that Violet Winterbottom's needle didn't even have thread.

Mrs. Highwood sniffed. Although the day was mild, she fanned herself with vigor. "Well, Miss Finch, perhaps this place can do my Diana some good." She looked to her eldest daughter. "We've seen all the best doctors, tried ever so many treatments. I even took her to Bath for the cure."

Susanna gave a sympathetic nod. From what she could gather, Diana Highwood had suffered bouts of mild asthma from a young age. With flaxen hair and a shy, rosy curve of a smile, the eldest Miss Highwood was a true beauty. Her fragile health had delayed what most certainly would be a stunning ton debut. However, Susanna strongly suspected the many doctors and treatments were what kept the young lady feeling ill.

She offered Diana a friendly smile. "I'm certain a stay in Spindle Cove will be of great benefit to Miss Highwood's health. Of great benefit to you all, for that matter."

In recent years, Spindle Cove had become the seaside destination of choice for a certain type of well-bred young lady: the sort no one knew what to do with. They included the sickly, the scandalous, and the painfully shy; young wives disenchanted with matrimony and young girls too enchanted with the wrong men . . . All of them delivered here by the guardians to whom they presented problems, in hopes that the sea air would cure them of their ills.

As the only daughter of the only local gentleman, Susanna was the village hostess by default. These awkward young ladies no one knew what to do with . . . she knew what to do with them. Or rather, she knew what not to do with them. No "cures" were necessary. They didn't need doctors pressing lancets to their veins, or finishing school matrons harping on their diction. They just needed a place to be themselves.

Spindle Cove was that place.

Mrs. Highwood worked her fan. "I'm a widow with no

sons, Miss Finch. One of my daughters must marry well, and soon. I've had such hopes for Diana, lovely as she is. But if she's not stronger by next season . . ." She made a dismissive wave toward her middle daughter, who sat in dark, bespectacled contrast to her fair-haired sisters. "I shall have no choice but to bring out Minerva instead."

"But Minerva doesn't care about men," young Charlotte said helpfully. "She prefers dirt and rocks."

"It's called geology," Minerva said. "It's a science."

"It's certain spinsterhood, is what it is! Unnatural girl. Do sit straight in your chair, at least." Mrs. Highwood sighed and fanned harder. To Susanna, she said, "I despair of her, truly. This is why Diana must get well, you see. Can you imagine Minerva in society?"

Susanna bit back a smile, all too easily imagining the scene. It would probably resemble her own debut. Like Minerva, she had been absorbed in unladylike pursuits, and the object of her female relations' oft-voiced despair. At balls, she'd been that freckled Amazon in the corner, who would have been all too happy to blend into the wallpaper, if only her hair color would have allowed it.

As for the gentlemen she'd met . . . not a one of them had managed to sweep her off her feet. To be fair, none of them had tried very hard.

She shrugged off the awkward memories. That time was behind her now.

Mrs. Highwood's gaze fell on a book at the corner of the table. "I am gratified to see you keep *Mrs. Worthington* close at hand."

"Oh yes," Susanna replied, reaching for the blue, leather-bound tome. "You'll find copies of *Mrs. Worthington's Wisdom* scattered everywhere throughout the village. We find it a very useful book."

"Hear that, Minerva? You would do well to learn it by heart." When Minerva rolled her eyes, Mrs. Highwood said, "Charlotte, open it now. Read aloud the beginning of Chapter Twelve."

Charlotte reached for the book and opened it, then cleared her throat and read aloud in a dramatic voice. "'Chapter Twelve. The perils of excessive education. A young lady's intellect should be in all ways like her undergarments. Present, pristine, and imperceptible to the casual observer.'"

Mrs. Highwood harrumphed. "Yes. Just so. Hear and believe it, Minerva. Hear and believe every word. As Miss Finch says, you will find that book very useful."

Susanna took a leisurely sip of tea, swallowing with it a bitter lump of indignation. She wasn't an angry or resentful person, as a matter of course. But once provoked, her passions required formidable effort to conceal.

That book provoked her, no end.

Mrs. Worthington's Wisdom for Young Ladies was the bane of sensible girls the world over, crammed with insipid, damaging advice on every page. Susanna could have gleefully crushed its pages to powder with a mortar and pestle, labeled the vial with a skull and crossbones, and placed it on the highest shelf in her stillroom, right beside the dried foxglove leaves and deadly nightshade berries.

Instead, she'd made it her mission to remove as many copies as possible from circulation. A sort of quarantine. Former residents of the Queen's Ruby sent the books from all corners of

England. One couldn't enter a room in Spindle Cove without finding a copy or three of *Mrs. Worthington's Wisdom*. And just as Susanna had told Mrs. Highwood, they found the book very useful indeed. It was the perfect size for propping a window open. It also made an excellent doorstop or paperweight. Susanna used her personal copies for pressing herbs. Or, occasionally, for target practice.

She motioned to Charlotte. "May I?" Taking the volume from the girl's grip, she raised the book high. Then, with a brisk thwack, she used it to crush a bothersome gnat.

With a calm smile, she placed the book on a side table. "Very useful indeed."

"THEY'LL NEVER KNOW what hit them." With his boot heel, Colin tamped a divot over the first powder charge.

"Nothing's going to hit them," Bram said. "We're not using shells."

The last thing they needed was shrapnel zinging about. The charges he prepared were mere blanks—black powder wrapped in paper, for a bit of noise and a spray of dirt.

"You're certain the horses won't bolt?" Colin asked, unspooling a length of slow-burning fuse.

"These are cavalry-trained beasts. Impervious to explosions. The sheep, on the other hand . . ."

"Will scatter like flies." Colin flashed a reckless grin.

"I suppose."

Bram knew bombing the sheep was reckless, impulsive, and inherently rather stupid, like all his cousin's boyhood ideas.

Surely there were better, more efficient solutions to a sheep barricade that didn't involve black powder.

But time was wasting, and Bram was impatient to be moving on, in more ways than one. Eight months ago, a lead ball had ripped through his right knee and torn his life apart. He'd spent months confined to a sickbed, another several weeks clanking and groaning his way down corridors like a ghost dragging chains. Some days during his convalescence, Bram had felt certain he would explode.

And now he was so close—just a mile or so—from Summerfield and Sir Lewis Finch. Just a mile from finally regaining his command. He bloody well wouldn't be thwarted by a flock of gluttonous sheep, whose guts were likely to burst if they weren't scared off that corn.

A good, clean blast was just what they all needed right about now.

"That'll do," Thorne called, embedding the last charge at the top of the rise. As he pushed his way back through the sheep, he added, "All's clear down the lane. I could see a fair distance."

"There is a village nearby, isn't there?" Colin asked. "God, tell me there's a village."

"There's a village," Bram answered, packing away the unused powder. "Saw it on the map. Somesuch Bay, or Whatsit Harbor . . . Can't exactly recall."

"I don't care what it's called," Colin said. "So long as there's a tavern and a bit of society. God, I hate the country."

Thorne said, "I saw the village. Just over that rise."

"It didn't look charming, did it?" Colin raised a brow as he reached for the tinderbox. "I should hate for it to be charming.

Give me a dank, seedy, vice-ridden pustule of a village any day. Wholesome living makes my skin crawl."

The corporal gave him a stony look. "I wouldn't know about charming, my lord."

"Yes. I can see that," Colin muttered. He struck a flint and lit the fuse. "Fair enough."

"MISS FINCH, WHAT a charming village." Diana Highwood clasped her hands together.

"We think so." Smiling modestly, Susanna led her guests onto the village green. "Here we have the church, St. Ursula's— a prized example of medieval architecture. Of course, the green itself is lovely." She refrained from pointing out the grass oval they used for cricket and lawn bowls, and quickly swiveled Mrs. Highwood away, lest she spy the pair of stockinged legs dangling from one of the trees.

"Look up there." She pointed out a jumble of stone arches and turrets decorating the rocky bluff.

"Those are the ruins of Rycliff Castle. They make an excellent place to paint and sketch."

"Oh, how perfectly romantic." Charlotte sighed.

"It looks damp," Mrs. Highwood pronounced.

"Not at all. In a month's time, the castle will be the site of our midsummer fair. Families come from ten parishes, some from as far away as Eastbourne. We ladies dress in medieval attire, and my father puts on a display for the local children. He collects ancient suits of armor, you see. Among other things."

"What a delightful notion," Diana said.

"It's the highlight of our summer."

Minerva peered hard at the bluffs. "What's the composition of those cliffs? Are they sandstone or chalk?"

"Er . . . sandstone, I think." Susanna directed their attention to a red-shuttered façade across the lane. Wide window boxes spilled over with blossoms, and a gilt-lettered sign swung noiselessly in the breeze. "And there's the tea shop. Mr. Fosbury, the proprietor, makes cakes and sweets to rival any London confectionery's."

"Cakes?" Mrs. Highwood's mouth pursed in an unpleasant manner. "I do hope you aren't indulging in an excess of sweets."

"Oh no," Susanna lied. "Hardly ever."

"Diana has been strictly forbidden to indulge. And that one"—she pointed out Minerva—"is tending toward stoutness, I fear."

At her mother's slight, Minerva turned her gaze to her feet, as if she were intently studying the pebbles beneath them. Or as if she were begging the ground to swallow her whole.

"*Minerva*," her mother snapped. "Posture."

Susanna put an arm about the young woman, shoring her up. "We have the sunniest weather in all England, did I mention that? The post comes through two times a week. Can I interest you all in a tour of the shops?"

"Shops? I only see one."

"Well, yes. There is only one. But it's all we have need of, you see. Bright's All Things shop has everything a young lady could wish to buy."

Mrs. Highwood surveyed the street. "Where is the doctor? Diana must have a doctor nearby at all times, to bleed her when she has her attacks."

Susanna winced. No wonder Diana's health never fully returned. Such a useless, horrific practice, bleeding. A "remedy" more likely to drain life than preserve it, and one Susanna had barely survived herself. Out of habit, she adjusted her long, elbow-length gloves. Their seams chafed against the well-healed scars beneath.

"There is a surgeon next town over," she said. A surgeon she wouldn't allow near cattle, much less a young lady. "Here in the village, we have a very capable apothecary." She hoped the woman would not ask for specifics there.

"What about men?" Mrs. Highwood asked.

"Men?" Susanna echoed. "What about them?"

"With so many unwed ladies in residence, are you not overrun with fortune hunters? Bath was teeming with them, all of them after my Diana's dowry. As if she would marry some smooth-talking third son."

"Definitely not, Mrs. Highwood." On this point, Susanna need not fudge. "There are no debt-ridden rakes or ambitious officers here. In fact, there are very few men in Spindle Cove at all. Aside from my father, only tradesmen and servants."

"I just don't know," Mrs. Highwood sighed, looking about the village once again. "It's all rather common, isn't it? My cousin, Lady Agatha, told me of a new spa in Kent. Mineral baths, purging treatments. Her ladyship swears by their mercury cure."

Susanna's stomach lurched. If Diana Highwood landed in a spa like that, it might truly be the end of her. "Please, Mrs. Highwood. One cannot underestimate the healthful benefits of simple sea air and sunshine."

Charlotte tugged her gaze from the ruined castle long

enough to plead, "Do let's stay, Mama. I want to take part in the midsummer fair."

"I believe I feel better already," Diana said, breathing deep.

Susanna left Minerva's side and approached the anxious matriarch. Mrs. Highwood might be a misguided, overwrought sort of woman, but she obviously loved her daughters and had their best interests at heart. She only needed a bit of reassurance that she was doing the right thing.

Well, Susanna could give her that reassurance truthfully. All three of the Highwood sisters needed this place. Diana needed a reprieve from quack medical treatments. Minerva needed a chance to pursue her own interests without censure. Young Charlotte just needed a place to be a girl, to stretch her growing legs and imagination.

And Susanna needed the Highwoods, for reasons she couldn't easily explain. She had no way to go back in time and undo the misfortunes of her own youth. But she could help to spare other young ladies the same friendless misery, and that was the next best thing.

"Trust me, Mrs. Highwood," she said, taking the woman's hand. "Spindle Cove is the perfect place for your daughters' summer holiday. I promise you, here they will be healthy, happy, and perfectly safe."

Boom. A distant blast punched the air. Susanna's ribs shivered with the force of it.

Mrs. Highwood clutched her bonnet with a gloved hand. "My word. Was that an explosion?"

Drat, drat, drat. And this had all been going so well.

"Miss Finch, you just claimed this place was safe."

"Oh, it is." Susanna gave them her most calming, reassuring

smile. "It is. No doubt that's just a ship in the Channel, sounding its signal cannon."

She knew very well there was no ship. That blast could only be her father's doing. In his day, Sir Lewis Finch had been a celebrated innovator of firearms and artillery. His contributions to the British Army had earned him acclaim, influence, and a sizable fortune. But after those incidents with the experimental cannon, he'd promised Susanna he would give up conducting field tests.

He'd *promised*.

As they moved forward into the lane, a strange, low rumble gathered in the air.

"What is that noise?" Diana asked.

Susanna feigned innocence. "What noise?"

"*That* noise," Mrs. Highwood said.

The rumble grew more forceful with each second. The paving stones vibrated beneath her heeled slippers. Mrs. Highwood squeezed her eyes shut and emitted a low, mournful whimper.

"Oh, *that* noise," Susanna said lightly, herding the Highwoods across the lane. If she could only get them indoors . . . "That noise is nothing to be concerned about. We hear it all the time here. A fluke of the weather."

"It cannot be thunder," Minerva said.

"No. No, it's not thunder. It's . . . an atmospheric phenomenon, brought on by intermittent gusts of . . ."

"Sheep!" Charlotte cried, pointing down the lane.

A flock of deranged, woolly beasts stormed through the ancient stone arch and poured into the village, funneling down the lane and bearing down on them.

"Oh yes," Susanna muttered. "Precisely so. Intermittent

gusts of sheep."

She hurried her guests across the lane, and they huddled in the All Things shop's doorway while the panicked sheep passed. The chorus of agitated bleats grated against her eardrums. If her father had hurt himself, she was going to kill him.

"There's no cause for alarm," Susanna said over the din. "Rural life does have its peculiar charms. Miss Highwood, is your breathing quite all right?"

Diana nodded. "I'm fine, thank you."

"Then won't you please excuse me?"

Without waiting for an answer, Susanna lifted her hem and made a mad dash down the lane, weaving around the few lingering sheep as she made her way straight out of the village. It didn't take but a matter of seconds. This was, after all, a very small village.

Rather than take the longer, winding lane around the hill, she climbed it. As she neared the top, the breeze delivered to her a few lingering wisps of smoke and scattered tufts of wool. Despite these ominous signs, she crested the hill to find a scene that did not resemble one of her father's artillery tests. Down at the bottom of the lane, two carts were stalled in the road. When she squinted, she could make out figures milling around the stopped conveyances. Tall, male figures. No short, stout, balding gentlemen among them.

None of them could be Papa.

She took a relieved gulp of acrid, powder-tinged air. With the burden of dread lifted, her curiosity took the fore. Intrigued, she picked her way down the bank of heather until she stood on the narrow, rutted road. In the distance, the figures of the men ceased moving. They'd noticed her.

Shading her brow with one hand, she peered hard at the men, trying to make out their identities. One of the men wore an officer's coat. Another wore no coat at all. As she approached them, the coatless man began to wave with vigor. Shouts carried up to her on the breeze. Frowning, Susanna moved closer, hoping to better hear the words.

"Wait! Miss, don't . . . !"

Whomp.

An unseen force plucked her straight off her feet and slammed her sideways, driving her off the lane entirely. She plowed shoulder-first into the tall grass, tackled to the turf by some kind of charging beast.

A charging beast wearing lobster-red wool.

Together, they bounced away from the road, elbows and knees absorbing the blows. Susanna's teeth rattled in her skull, and she bit her tongue hard. Fabric ripped, and cool air reached farther up her thigh than any well-mannered breeze ought to venture.

When they rolled to a stop, she found herself pinned by a tremendous, huffing weight. And pierced by an intense green gaze.

"Wh—?" Her breath rushed out in question.

Boom, the world answered.

Susanna ducked her head, burrowing into the protection of what she'd recognized to be an officer's coat. The knob of a brass button pressed into her cheek. The man's bulk formed a comforting shield as a shower of dirt clods rained down on them both. He smelled of whiskey and gunpowder.

After the dust cleared, she brushed the hair from his brow, searching his gaze for signs of confusion or pain. His eyes were alert and intelligent, and still that startling shade of green—as hard and richly hued as jade.

She asked, "Are you well?"

"Yes." His voice was a deep rasp. "Are you?"

She nodded, expecting him to release her at the confirmation. When he showed no signs of moving, she puzzled at it. Either he was gravely injured or seriously impertinent. "Sir, you're . . . er, you're rather heavy." Surely he could not fail to miss *that* hint.

He replied, "You're soft."

Good Lord. Who was this man? Where had he come from? And how was he still *atop* her?

"You have a small wound." With trembling fingers, she brushed a reddish knot high on his temple, near his hairline. "Here." She pressed her hand to his throat, feeling for his pulse. She found it, thumping strong and steady against her gloved fingertips.

"Ah. That's nice."

Her face blazed with heat. "Are you seeing double?"

"Perhaps. I see two lips, two eyes, two flushed cheeks . . . a thousand freckles."

She stared at him.

"Don't concern yourself, miss. It's nothing." His gaze darkened with some mysterious intent. "Nothing a little kiss won't mend."

And before she could even catch her breath, he pressed his lips to hers.

A kiss. His mouth, touching hers. It was warm and firm, and then . . . it was over.

Her first real kiss in all her five-and-twenty years, and it was finished in a heartbeat. Just a memory now, save for the faint bite of whiskey on her lips. And the heat. She still tasted his scorching, masculine heat. Belatedly, she closed her eyes.

"There, now," he murmured. "All better."

Better? Worse? The darkness behind her eyelids held no answers, so she opened them again.

Different. This strange, strong man held her in his protective embrace, and she was lost in his intriguing green stare, and his kiss reverberated in her bones with more force than a powder blast. And now she felt different.

The heat and weight of him . . . they were like an answer. The answer to a question Susanna hadn't even been aware her body was asking. So this was how it would be, to lie beneath a man. To feel shaped by him, her flesh giving in some places and resisting in others. Heat building between two bodies; dueling heartbeats pounding both sides of the same drum.

Maybe . . . just maybe . . . this was what she'd been waiting to feel all her life. Not swept her off her feet—but flung across the lane and sent tumbling head over heels while the world exploded around her.

Want to read more? Order now!

http://tessadare.com/?p=2215

Other Books by Tessa

Castles Ever After series

Romancing the Duke

Say Yes to the Marquess – releases December 30, 2014

Spindle Cove series

A Night to Surrender

Once Upon a Winter's Eve

A Week to be Wicked

A Lady by Midnight

Beauty and the Blacksmith

Any Duchess Will Do

Not part of a series

The Scandalous, Dissolute, No-Good Mr. Wright

Stud Club trilogy

One Dance with a Duke

Twice Tempted by a Rogue

Three Nights with a Scoundrel

Wanton Dairymaid trilogy

Goddess of the Hunt

Surrender of a Siren

A Lady of Persuasion

About the Author

Tessa Dare is the *New York Times* and *USA Today* bestselling author of eleven historical romance novels and four novellas. Her books have won numerous accolades, including Romance Writers of America's prestigious RITA® award and multiple *RT Book Reviews* Reviewer's Choice Awards. *Booklist* magazine named her one of the "new stars of historical romance," and her books have been contracted for translation in more than a dozen languages.

A librarian by training and a booklover at heart, Tessa makes her home in Southern California, where she lives with her husband, their two children and a big brown dog.

To learn more, please visit www.tessadare.com or join Tessa's mailing list (tessadare.com/newsletter-signup/) to be notified of her upcoming releases.

57315722R00059

Made in the USA
Lexington, KY
11 November 2016